Shadows in the Tree

Shadows in the Tree is an inviting and riveting story . . . DeBruin most skillfully explores the emotional toll on women and their families as they leave behind all they knew and face a dangerous and unknown future . . . I heartily recommend this book to anyone wanting to examine the human experience of many a Loyalist refugee.
— *The Loyalist Gazette*, review by Grietje R. McBride, UE, B Sc.

* * *

Thank you for taking me on another incredible journey with Eliza. It is a *powerful* and *emotional* journey. What I can only begin to imagine, you put into words and make images so vivid in my mind that I felt like I was on the trail with Maria Catrina. I cried and rejoiced along with her. Congratulations Jennifer, the book is wonderful . . . It truly is a heartfelt story and I know that others will feel it as deeply as I did. — S. Seymour

My sister just gave me your second book, *Shadows in the Tree*. Jennifer, I couldn't put it down. You are truly a gifted writer. You make the reader a participant in the story, a reader who is transported all those years ago to share in the joys and trials of the times. Thank you once again for a brilliant novel and I am looking forward to your next book. Keep them coming. — M. Craig

I just finished reading your second book and had to tell you how much I enjoyed it. Your descriptions of scenery and events were good, but those of the heroine's emotions, exceptional. You brought reality and drama to the pages. — Sheila H.

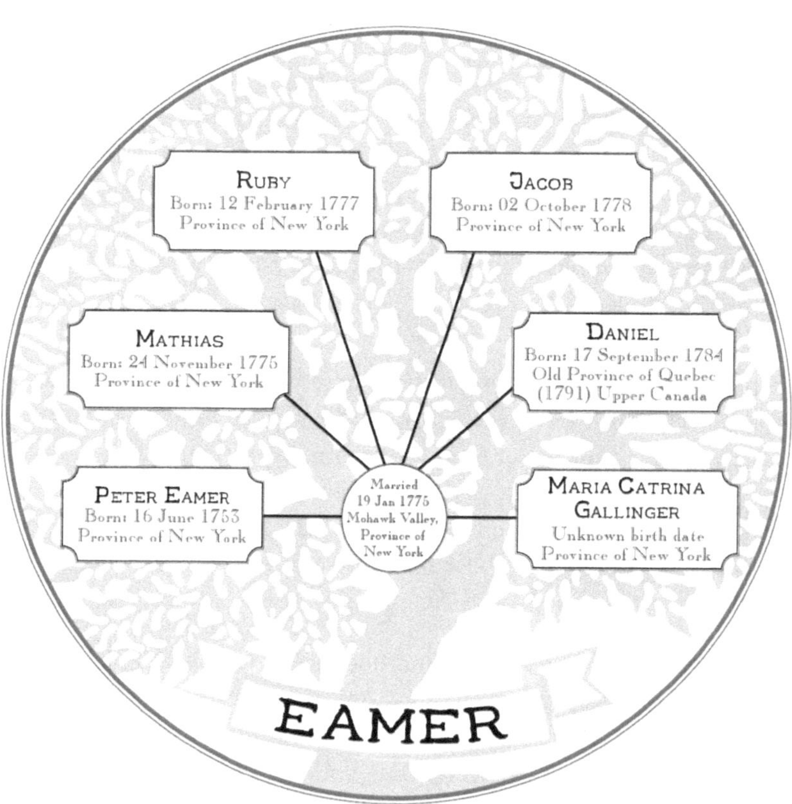

RUBY
Born: 12 February 1777
Province of New York

JACOB
Born: 02 October 1778
Province of New York

MATHIAS
Born: 24 November 1775
Province of New York

DANIEL
Born: 17 September 1784
Old Province of Quebec
(1791) Upper Canada

PETER EAMER
Born: 16 June 1753
Province of New York

Married
19 Jan 1775
Mohawk Valley,
Province of
New York

MARIA CATRINA
GALLINGER
Unknown birth date
Province of New York

EAMER

SHADOWS IN THE TREE

JENNIFER DeBruin UE

Published by Jennifer DeBruin
www.jenniferdebruin.com

ISBN 978-0-9947461-1-5 (pbk.)
978-0-9947461-6-0 (EPUB)
978-0-9947461-7-7 (MOBI)

For my loyal ancestors —
especially the grandmothers who linger in the shadows of history.

PROLOGUE

Rocking slowly in front of an open fireplace of large grey river rock . . . orange, yellow, and occasional blue flames dancing about . . . dark orange-red coals glowing within the centre . . . crackling of cedar wood, creating sparks that fly about on the hearth . . . the strong, comforting smell of the smoke escaping and floating upwards along the face of the rocks . . . long skirt making a swishing sound with every movement . . .

Looking down, gently rubbing the curve of my belly, expanding ever so slightly, taking on a familiar roundness.

"Mine own."

ELIZA AND DAVID sat at the kitchen table in the quiet of the early dawn, enjoying their coffee, before the children woke. Finally breaking the silence, she said, "I dreamt I was pregnant last night."

In a flash, David looked up at her, with an expression that could only be described as chagrin.

Eliza laughed. David always "freaked out" when she had dreamt of being pregnant in the past. Happy with the two children they had, neither had felt the urge to have more, but from time to time, Eliza still dreamt of it. "The only weird thing is, I don't think it was me. I was someone else. I had on a long, old-fashioned skirt—I think," she said, pausing, remembering the details, " —and I was rocking in front of an open fireplace; you know, the kind that has the big fieldstones or river rock. It was so vivid."

"Well, as long as you *aren't* pregnant, that's the main thing," David said, smiling weakly at her.

Eliza laughed at his half-joking tone. "You never did get over diaper changes and nighttime feedings, did you?"

"No," came the serious reply, which told Eliza both were still very fresh in David's memory.

CHAPTER 1

I CAN'T WAIT until I can sleep in again, Eliza thought, peering at the clock, trying to comprehend that morning had in fact come again so soon. *Okay, only twelve days until the end of the semester—you can do it, Eliza,* she whispered under her breath, trying to muster the energy to get out of bed. While she loved being a college professor, after a busy semester she was looking forward to no longer waking in the dark of early mornings, necessitated by her hour-long drive to the campus. Crawling out of bed, still in a daze of fighting the need to wake, she made her way to the window to check the weather. She was glad to see the familiar glow on the horizon that was showing the signs of a nice spring day.

Settling in for the long drive, coffee at the ready to help fuel the energy needed to keep up with her students, Eliza, inspired by the first peek of the sun above the horizon and the fact that she had made it out the door earlier than expected, decided not to take her usual route along the major highway and instead enjoy the more meandering drive down Highway 2, along the St. Lawrence River. Although at least twenty minutes longer, it was worth it to experience the "magic" of the river, which was most palpable in the morning as the world slowly shook off its slumber.

There's another one. Eliza took note of the many Loyalist flags that flew in front of historic, and some not-so-historic, dwellings along this riverfront drive. While she knew she, too, was descended from the Loyalists, she did not know much about them beyond anecdotal facts from her occasional visits to museums. Even with this limited knowledge, she did know it was over 220 years after their arrival and wondered, *Why do these people, obviously descendants, hold so steadfastly to commemorating something so long ago in the past?*

This was just the kind of question she was looking forward to answering. A brief foray into exploring her connection to this river a decade earlier had led to an interest in genealogy. As she succumbed to the intrigue and excitement of finding these connections and stories within her own family tree, she became interested in finding out her links to the Loyalists. Not only was it the flags that still flew so proudly, but the river itself seemed to hold in its deep waters the secrets of millennia. Cutting through the landscape from the Atlantic Ocean to the Great Lakes, it had the experiences of so many within her own family tied to it.

Magic. Glancing at the river just a few feet and a precarious drop away from her on the narrow road, Eliza turned from thoughts of her Loyalist connections and looked at the waters that now captured her imagination. It was now just half an hour after sunrise, and the mists floated from the river, dissipating in the brightening morning sky. Geese and ducks that had taken refuge in the safety of the waters for the night were now flying in groups, often fading into the haze created by the river's mist. The water, quiet and still in parts, reflected the images of the flying birds and sky like a mirror, making it seem like there was no beginning or end to the river. The only detectable movement was the occasional splash in the water, or evidence of ripples created by the creatures that called the water itself home.

With very few people yet beginning their daily routine, this always seemed to be the river's own time in a world that bustled about it, perhaps even becoming an invisible backdrop to daily life once the day was in full swing. But early in the morning, before the world awoke, the river continued with its ancient rituals, welcoming back the geese that had flown to warmer destinations during the cold winter months; life was abounding from its depths, and the cool river waters were warmed by the rising sun . . . *magic*. With windows down and radio off, the sounds of geese greeting the day with their honking and birds singing their melodic tunes were always a wonderful way to gain a sense of calm and connection to something bigger, older, and wiser than the stresses and routine of day-to-day life. As a laker became visible through the mists just downriver, Eliza knew the river's time alone was ending for another day.

Already planning her genealogy project for the summer, Eliza, keeping one eye on the road, pulled out her ever-present notebook and pen and jotted down a short, scrawled notation: *find out more about my Loyalist ancestors*. With this simple note, Eliza set herself on a course that would take her on a journey more than 200 years into her own past.

CHAPTER 2

WHAT SECRETS ARE YOU HIDING FROM ME? With the hectic term over, Eliza focused on her personal project of solving this latest mystery in her family tree. Typing her grandfather's name, Frederick Eamer, into her genealogy program, Eliza's grandparents' file appeared. Her grandfather was the entry point to a web of German Palatines, a people she knew little about. With sparse information beyond this generation, she began her search online hoping one of the multitude of ancestry sites would yield clues. Querying "Eamer, Loyalist," the first hit was a Peter Eamer, UE. Quickly looking up what UE stood for, she discovered it was "the honorific title for a proven United Empire Loyalist, and their descendants." Intrigued at the possibility of being added to this list, she put a star beside the notation: *find proof!*

Oh, no, it's gone. Navigating the sketchy information on Peter Eamer, Eliza was disheartened to find a map showing that the land Peter had been granted for his loyalty to the king during the American Revolution was now lost to history under the waters of the St. Lawrence River. She found her thoughts wandering to the lost homesteads, villages, battlefields . . . and graveyards.

This was a story Eliza knew well, as her grandmother, Mary, had grown up in the "lost village" of Moulinette, one of the many historic places flooded during the 1950s Seaway and power dam construction. But not only were places lost forever; so were people. Overcome by the memory of her grandmother's grief in relating her story of this loss, Eliza could still hear Mary's voice: "The last time I went to see Mama, I had to remember where she was because they had taken her stone away; they had taken all the stones away. I never forgot, you know. Even without any markers left, the villages gone, no trees, gardens, or houses . . . I never forgot where Mama was."

Mary's beloved "Mama" died during the tuberculosis pandemic of the 1930s, and her grave, along with many others, could not be moved from its final resting place. Buried once again by the waters that now flowed over them, there was no place to mourn except to look over the beautiful source of their despair and remember what once was. It was evident in the telling that Mary had felt the raw emotions of this dramatic and gut-wrenching experience as vividly at the end of her life as she had when it was happening. Even more despairing was the way in which she told it — not as an adult, but as the fourteen-year-old girl she was when she lost her.

Any tangible evidence of Peter's existence is lost, Eliza thought, imagining an old gravestone askew somewhere at the bottom of the river.

Well, who do we have here? "Wife of Peter Eamer, Maria Catrina. Married 19 Jan 1775 in the Province of New York. Of German Palatine descent, she was the daughter of Michael Gallinger." Unable to find a reliable birth date for her, Eliza was not surprised, as women in her family tree were generally found as simple notations of "daughter of . . . wife of . . . mother of . . ." This entry merely confirmed the tradition of tracing families primarily through male lines, and she, too, was guilty of this. Eliza found that seeking out the most easily found answers first, those generally related to the men, created a sense of motivation. Early in her budding interest in genealogy, her intention was to also discover the details of the women in her family tree; but days spent in fruitless pursuit of answers was frustrating and lessened the "fun" of playing genealogical detective, so this was quickly abandoned.

Tracing the Eamers back through the generations to their emigration to the "American colony," Eliza was caught up in the romance of the journey that played out in the information before her: Old sailing ships crossing the ocean; hundreds of people carrying their worldly goods in just a few heavy canvas bags and old wooden crates, taking wagons across untamed land at the very edge of the frontier, which the Mohawk Valley was at the time, and carving out small farms with wooden cabins. The descriptions of the interactions and challenges of these newcomers living among the Iroquois on their traditional lands were, Eliza thought, *very romantic indeed, with all the elements of a good, classic, early-American story.* Reflecting on the story of these German Palatines, her romanticized imagination became fired with the old, familiar obsession to learn even more of the story of her ancestors . . . but this would not be like the last time.

That night, after her children had gone to bed and her husband, David, had settled in front of the TV, Eliza took a few moments at her desk, transcribing the information she had gained on her first day of researching the life of Peter Eamer. As she filled in the details of her genealogy, Eliza felt a growing sense of regret and loss, similar to—*no*, she was sure—it was the feeling of having a broken heart, a feeling she had not had since before meeting David sixteen years earlier.

On the day she started recording data on the children of Peter and Maria Catrina, the feeling was particularly strong, almost overwhelming. Brushing it off as being overtired from the long hours at her desk and the restless sleep she had been having over the past few nights, Eliza's logical mind fought against the illogical feelings she was having . . . but couldn't shake them.

Soon settling into bed with the intention of reading a good book for the remainder of the evening, Eliza fell asleep after only a few pages.

. . . Looking down, gently rubbing the curve of my belly, expanding ever so slightly, taking on a familiar roundness . . .

"Mine own."

CHAPTER 3

*D*ark.

"Where are you?"

Frantically pleading, "Where are you?"

A little figure darts ahead out of reach. "Come back!" Running toward the little one, tree branches hitting my face, can't catch it, too far ahead. "Stop!" Can't see anything in the darkness. "Where are you?"

Dark. No sound. Strong smell of pine. Cold. Desperation. "Where are you?" No response. Dark.

"Mine own."

"ELIZA, WAKE UP." As she came to, she heard crying, only to realize it was her own. David was sitting up, gently pushing her to wake her from the nightmare. "Eliza, are you okay? You were crying."

Eliza slowly regained her senses. "I dreamt I lost one of the kids. I don't know which one it was; I could see them ahead of me, but he—or she—was far away and it was really dark," she renewed her crying, feeling the full impact of this type of fear. The fear all parents have in the thought of losing a child. "I tried running to them, but I was sort of stuck, like I was in slow motion. It was so dark I couldn't see where I was. I think I was outside, because I was cold."

"You were shivering," David said as he drew Eliza to him, laying her head on his chest and pulling the duvet up around her shoulders.

Slowly taking comfort in his arms, Eliza said, "I haven't

dreamt of losing the kids since they were babies. It's so weird. I heard a voice just as you woke me up. Did you say 'mine own'?"

"No. I said, 'Wake up.' That's it."

"I think I'll go check on the kids. I'll sleep better knowing they're safe and sound." Eliza rose from the warmth of her bed, still feeling the chill from her dream, and wrapped her housecoat tightly around her, as much for warmth as for comfort. She made her way to each of the kids' rooms, as she had when previously disturbed by dreams, and was assured both were where they were supposed to be.

Crawling back under the covers of her own bed, she tried to resume her sleep, only to find the images of her dream still fresh every time she shut her eyes. Realizing it was futile to struggle with sleep while feeling this sense of panic that lingered, she turned on the TV, finally falling asleep with the din of the noise to occupy her mind.

Generally, in the light of day, the feelings of her vivid dreams would dissipate, but not this time. Eliza found herself unable to shake the fear she had experienced the night before. The dreams, though fragmented, were so vivid. She couldn't remember ever having had all the faculties of her senses be so engaged, and never had she been able to recall them in such detail. They remained with her as memories, more than just vague snippets, as was the usual case. She had dreamt of losing her kids in a store before, a common dream of most mothers, but this was outside, and she didn't really recognize the setting, except she remembered the cold, which made her shiver even now at the thought of it. The element that was most confusing her was not being able to make sense of the pieces because she continued to feel as though she were not herself but someone else. A pattern was also emerging in that she was always hearing in a melancholy, whispered voice, "mine own," which ended each night's dream with a suddenness of expecting to see the source of the voice.

Finally gathering her thoughts to the task at hand, she set about finalizing the Eamer file, before moving on to the American Revolution itself. Throughout the morning, the memory of the whispered voice was ever-present in her mind . . . "mine own."

Transcribing the notes of Peter and Maria Catrina's children, she soon got lost in the data entry and was able to shake off the feelings she had been having. First was Mathias, born 24 November 1775; second, Ruby, 12 February 1777; third, Jacob, 2 October 1778; but as she entered the name of the fourth child, Daniel, 17 September 1784, she heard "mine own" quite clearly behind her. She turned to look, fully expecting to see someone, but there was no one. It was the first time she had "heard" it while awake. Sitting for a few moments trying to gather her thoughts, Eliza realized that the intensity of the feelings, the "hearing" of a voice, and in particular the dreams, were the strongest phenomena she had ever experienced while doing her research. She had, of course, on more than one occasion found herself saddened by the stories of her ancestors — who wouldn't be, learning of women dying in childbirth, or having multiple children die at times of widespread disease? But this was different. *This seems so real.*

When Eliza had embarked upon learning about the Eamers, the beginning of her Loyalist connections, she believed the research into the American Revolution itself would be the most engaging and interesting part. Now, though, the focus was not the entire Eamer family, not just the wars and strife of the Loyalists. Time and again, she had felt the strongest feelings in relation to Peter specifically. *No*, she reflected, *not just Peter.* These were *maternal* feelings she was sensing so strongly. Maria Catrina was coming into sharper focus.

Eliza pulled out her notebook, making a quick notation for the next day's research: *Find out more about Maria Catrina Gallinger.* Satisfied with the work that had been accomplished so far, Eliza put away her Eamer family genealogy book and went to bed. But tonight would not bring the sound sleep she was so desperately seeking. It was the night the fragments of her dreams would knit together — the night she would begin to understand the true, heartbreaking meaning of "mine own."

CHAPTER 4

The world is wrapped in blinding, all-embracing light—the fog, thick as muslin, dispersing it. Radiant streaks of light shine like golden ribbons from the sky, reaching to the earth, while tufts of thicker fog drift by, weightless and ethereal. Is this heaven?

No horizon or sky visible . . . only light.

The only evidence of life in this light is the sounds of birds welcoming the day with their joyful, melodic chirps; otherwise, stillness and peace . . . a sense of being wrapped in an untouchable place and time. Though the warmth of the day has not yet arrived with the light, the sense of serenity warms and comforts the soul, briefly allowing for a moment to just "be."

Out past the rail fencing at the edge of the yard, I see him walking the fields, as he does every morning. Tall and straight, his golden hair is just catching glimmers of sun coming through the haze; the combination is making him seem almost unearthly. How handsome he is. He bends to check the dark, furrowed soil, taking a handful and letting it fall back to the earth whence it came. Just then, he turns his head and looks at me, still kneeling, and smiles. I cannot help but smile back. His hauntingly soft blue eyes, with just a hint of grey, seem as though they see right into my soul; my heart flutters. He stands and walks to meet me at the fenceline. I listen intently in the open door of the house to make sure the little occupant is still in a slumber. Assured, I step off the porch and make my way to him.

"Good morning, dearest."

I answer with a smile as I reach the fence. The grass is wet, and my bare feet feel the refreshing coolness of the dew. I lift my skirt, as the hem is brushing the ground.

"The fields are looking good. We will plant this week, and if all goes well, the harvest will be in on time." His voice is tinged with the slightest sense of scepticism.

"It *will* go well, I am sure of it," though in my heart I am not sure at all. Suddenly, I feel an overwhelming sense of foreboding and I try and push it to the back of my mind, not wanting to disturb this otherwise perfect morning.

"The growing discontent among our own little community is something that we must now take into consideration. The world is changing around us, and it seems we may be swept up in this change as well."

"What have you heard?"

"Just rumblings, but these grow ever louder by the day." As he looks at me with a serious expression on his face, I can see the concern. He notices my acknowledgement of this and takes my hand in his. It is warm, much warmer than mine. At the touch, he grabs both my hands. "You are cold." He wraps his hands around both of mine and warms them. "Better?"

"Yes, much better." The feeling of security takes hold again and thoughts of unsure, troubling things dissipate. "Let us take a walk to the river later; the fish are quite plentiful." I look toward the river, just beyond the farthest field. It is only now visible as the fog begins to lift. The dark water follows the twists and turns of its path and eventually disappears in the distance behind a stand of willow trees, displaying varying colours of green as newly sprouted leaves emerge.

Hearing faint crying coming from the open door of the house, we both look, turning to each other smiling. As I walk toward the house, I glance up at the window from which the intermittent crying is coming. The faded grey wood of the house makes the delicate pink blossoms on the apple tree close by seem all that much more vibrant. The world is slowly coming to life. I can feel him watching me . . . a comforting thought. As I pass into the darkened entryway, I turn one last time to look at him. His back is now turned to me and he is slowly walking back into the field, though he is looking toward the horizon, now fully revealing itself in the heat of the sun. Following his gaze, I can see the river winding like a shimmering, silver ribbon through the valley below, which is green and lush — and alive with the promise of a new season. *Yes, this must be heaven. All that I love is here.* As I shut the door behind me, I wonder if the world, now full of change and discontent, will soon come knocking on the door of my home.

"Mine own."

ELIZA WOKE, instinctively understanding that the dreams made further research unnecessary. Relinquishing her apprehension and need for logical explanation, she opened her heart to the story that was in the telling.

CHAPTER 5

May 20, 1776

... **K**nocks at the door, one after the other. No genial greetings as it opens and they walk in, the door shutting behind them quickly. He ushers them to the table, where they sit in silence, waiting until all have arrived.

Looking out the window into the darkness, I cannot see the men until they arrive at our door, and with every opening, I feel the bitter cold brush by me. The outer edges of the glass have an intricate pattern of frost slowly making its way over the entirety of each pane. Though cold for this late in the spring, it is beautiful, and for a moment I am mesmerized by the detail of the growing facets — then another knock at the door abruptly recaptures my attention, and the fear in the depths of my stomach returns.

He is sitting at the table with his father and three brothers discussing the days' events. As I look up from my spinning wheel across the room, careful to maintain the familiar rhythm and hum to disguise my listening in, I can plainly see his pensive look and furrowed brow, despite the poor lighting of the room, with now only a candle by my side and the dim firelight from the kitchen hearth to see by. "We must not bring attention to ourselves tonight, my dear," he had said earlier. I know he did not want to alarm me; I could tell from his gentle tone. But his face told me he was troubled, and I felt a pang of fear.

"Dear sons, we are now most truly on our own. There must be no attempt made to align ourselves in any way with either side. It is most prudent to maintain our neutrality in this conflict. Our every move and word will be monitored, particularly with the method by which the escape was made."

"Father, we have tried to maintain our neutrality, but we are ever more in a precarious position. Our neighbours demand that we arm against the government and the unreasonable taxation they force upon us. Upon the sudden departure of Sir John and many of our neighbours, I have just today received a visit asking that I join the rebel cause. Though our convictions are taken into account by those who know us, we must remember that others have now come to our doorstep who will not be so understanding of our position."

I see fear in his eyes. In this moment, though young, he has the troubled expression of a man much older, making him look much like his father sitting at the head of the table. Though his father, too, looks concerned, it is obvious he is sure in his conviction, which seems to provide some sense of calm.

"It is true, Peter. It may at times be difficult to resist the lure of this 'liberty' they speak of. I, too, feel the oppression of the taxation of a far-off master. Yet, we must not forget our place in this colony. If not for the generosity to our forefathers, we would be back in the motherland with no hope of a bright future. Here, we have been given the right to make a way for ourselves. Should we not honour our grandfathers for the efforts they made in providing this for us?"

"Yes," says Martin, the oldest of the brothers, sitting to my husband's left. "But if we are called to choose sides—if we *must* choose sides—we must stay as one. It seems more and more that we will not be able to wait it out. Too many of our neighbours have found their loyalties divided, with disastrous results."

Occasionally glancing up, I notice that all the faces look to their father for guidance. As I listen, terrifying thoughts come to mind. *What are we to do with a babe in arms if we are to flee as our neighbours and friends have done?* Looking out the window again, I cannot imagine a trek on such a cold, dark night. Even now, the fire, purposely allowed to die down, has left the room cold and penetrating, making it hard to grasp the wool now passing through my fingers. The roof cracks suddenly in protest to the cold that has settled upon it, and everyone jumps. Soon, I hear the faint rustling of my little one upstairs and put down my work, grabbing the candle at my side, to check.

I look upon him, asleep — my baby wrapped tightly in his warm blanket, like a cocoon of the butterflies that signal the return of warmer weather and happier times past. Staring at him, I feel the tug of heartstrings; the strength of such a connection, these six months since his birth, yet holds me in its wonder. Tonight, and the events of the past days, has renewed and heightened my fear for his safety — for his future. For now, he is unaware of the turmoil that surrounds us . . . invades our life and now defines our every word and movement. Thinking back to the discussion going on below reminds me that we are now unsure of whom we can trust. Dim fires and hushed tones now define our existence.

I hear the sounds of boots upon the wooden floor; the door creaks open and closes. I turn one last time to look upon the innocent. Assured that he is safe, for now, I slowly descend the stairs to face the fear that awaits me.

Standing by the hearth, his hand on the mantel, he is looking intently into the dim, glowing coals. Silent and still, I see he is brooding and concerned by the conversation. I do not want to disturb his thoughts so I silently make my way to the stool to resume my spinning. Just as I reach it, however, he looks over at me, eyes as penetrating as ever, but tonight with a definite lack of the brightness that generally looks upon me.

"I hope you were not too upset by our discussion," he says with a faint, sorrowful smile. A knowing glance between us tells me he is aware I was listening.

As I pull the shawl tighter around my shoulders, he notices and reaches for a log to reignite the fire and bring warmth once again to the house. "The little one sleeps well enough, I hope?"

"Yes, I have just been up to check, and he is fine."

"It is good he is too young to know of the ways of our world, for they are distressing indeed." He looks into the flames, thoughts of something dire obviously filling his mind as the furrow deepens upon his brow. I come up beside him, taking his hand in mine to ease his mind and bring him back from a solitary place. "I will protect you, you can be assured of that," he says, looking at me and then at the ceiling toward the place where our baby sleeps. I feel a sense of relief, though in my heart I know it may not be possible.

"Surely our friends and neighbours will come to their senses?" I say, without conviction.

"Surely," he replies absentmindedly, again back in that solitary place in his mind.

CHAPTER 6

July 11, 1776

"Liberty is ours!"

As the rider passes our home, I turn from my work in the flourishing garden to see Peter rushing to the path on which the rider comes, waving this man down to ask what news he has. With a broad, victorious smile, the man does not dismount, but says with an air of triumph, "It means, sir, the time of the king in these lands comes to an end."

"In what manner has this been accomplished?" My beloved sounds unconvinced that such a thing should be true.

"By way of the signing of a declaration confirmed by the Continental Congress just these seven days, which states we are to make our way in this world, and shall not abide by the regulations set upon us by an unjust master who knows little of our life in this place, yet demands our obedience and riches."

"And what proof do we have that this is so?" Peter minds his anger, as this messenger seems to wait for confrontation, for he knows us to be loyal to His Majesty's rule. We have long been marked as such, and no evidence of continuing to want peace among our own people will abate this sentiment.

"You may come to hear the news yourself, for upon this very day, this declaration will be read at Johnson Hall for all to celebrate—or heed as they will." In delivering his news—or warning—he looks toward me, nodding, having just noticed my presence, and rides off in a cloud of dust on the dry road. As he does so, he continues to announce his news: "Liberty is ours!"

With the midday sun above us, the oppressive heat of this July day brings work in the fields to an end until it subsides. As I retreat into the house to make Peter his meal, he follows and, obviously agitated, says, "I expect my father and brothers to arrive shortly." Our home has become the gathering point for our kin, as we are the farm closest to our community, and when much needed to be discussed after each visit to Johnstown, it was made necessary that our home should act as such. I was glad to have this be so, for I could remain aware of much of what was taking place; yet I often wondered if, in their ignorance of the news that I have heard over these many months, my sisters and mother-in-law were not to be envied.

The previous winter, my father-in-law had purchased Mr. Paine's pamphlet, *Common Sense*, for his sons to read that they might more fully understand the sentiments of so many of our neighbours. My beloved forbade me to read it, for he thought it too much for my gentle ways and would set unnecessary fear in my heart. As he put it many times: "My duty to discuss with my kin is so that I may keep you from harm, whether from the knowledge of it, or necessity it may cause." What he does not know is that my every waking hour — and dreams upon the night — are filled with fearsome things despite his efforts. As the discussions ensued, I often listened in, though I busied myself with knitting or mending, which provided the quiet to hear each word, yet appear as though I were not interested. I had abandoned spinning, with an early realization that it muffled their words, for, aware of my presence, they often spoke in hushed voices. I know it to be a sin, but I cannot help myself; and so I pray for the dear Lord to forgive my disobedience to my beloved and his instruction that I should not be concerned with such matters. The stories I have heard these many months leave me feeling that knowing of these matters may come to some use, if the unthinkable were to happen.

Soon a few carriages, men on horseback, and many neighbours afoot, begin to pass by our home. Most are in a jovial mood, much as a community celebration of old, although it has been many months since such levity has existed in our valley. Then, there are our people, who pass by with sombre disposition, yet their heads held high, not losing their dignity, even as others raced past, looking upon them with scorn. Of course, there are very few of our people; most of the people passing us are excitedly going to hear what they deem a victory over "tyranny."

As my beloved's kin begin to appear, I am surprised to see my sisters, and, most surprisingly, my mother-in-law. So many months have passed since I have had occasion to see them; I cannot stifle the tears that now flow freely, and see they do the same. I run to them, and, without restraint, we embrace each other, as the little ones run about. This is the most relief I have felt in many days; thoughts of why we gather seem to leave me for just a moment, and lightness and joy reappear . . . a welcome reprieve.

As I look toward Peter, confused as to why the womenfolk should be gathered, my father-in-law addresses our group: "This we must all hear, and perhaps in our numbers show we have not all been driven from our own lands; and that, despite this turn, we intend to stay and maintain our peaceful existence among our neighbours. Your mother shall tend to the children."

I am glad to have my husband's mother in my presence again. As she takes Mathias in her arms, she pulls me into a tender embrace. Whispering in my ear, so that I might be the only one to hear, she says, "Take heart, my dear, for our path is righteous and our God will surely protect us in these terrible times."

I am glad for her advice, for I feel very unsure about my safety in making this once-familiar journey. The thought of being surrounded by so many that we had called friend at one time sets fear in my heart as I realize we want opposing outcomes. And perhaps today I will hear their victory made real, and my hope for a future I dream of still, dashed upon the reading of this document.

My sisters and I walk in silence behind our husbands and father-in-law, who hold their heads high with the same dignity they have always shown. They are respected men of our community, even among those who celebrate this reading. Our men have always commanded respect for their wise and thoughtful manner. As they stride along, each tall and fair, broad shoulders side by side, they most certainly are men of distinction; for despite all the troubles, each man they pass pays them the respect of noblemen, giving deference to them and allowing us to pass. I pray this respect may be so upon the end of this day, for I feel exposed away from the protection of my home.

As we approach Johnson Hall, I see that many remain in our valley, though it is evident that our people are fewer than I had imagined. The rejoicing people of the group gather close to the steps of the home, where a podium has been placed for the reading. Laughter and songs of victory fill the air, but we do not join in. We move toward a group of sullen people, quietly set off to the side under the shade of the great trees of the estate. My sisters and I sit quickly down upon the ground, while the men greet each other with a serious nature and talk of what can be expected.

I am overwhelmed to see my mother and father appear from the crowd. I weep as a child, and am ashamed to do so, but cannot help myself. I stand just as my mother reaches for me. Embracing me, she strokes my hair, as she once did, softly singing to me the song I now sing to my own little one. I did not realize I needed such comfort as only my mother can provide. All too soon, we remember our place, and once again abide by the modesty expected of us. My father smiles broadly at me, as he continues to speak with my father-in-law about the reason for our gathering.

"What of my brothers and sisters, dear Mother?"

"Your oldest brothers, Johann and Christian, have fled with Sir John, taking their wives and children with them. I pray they have found their way to Quebec, which is where Sir John knows he will find aid in our plight. Of your other brothers and sisters who remain with us, they are in the care of Henrich, who is most serious in his nature, and will surely keep the others safe until our return."

Henrich I remember only as a boy of twelve years, and when I suddenly realize he would now be fourteen, and a young man, I understand most acutely the passing of time and the ache of separation.

As a distinguished man with a long, white beard appears from the doorway, our time together to learn news of loved ones is over, and my mother moves to rejoin my father, departing my company. My heart aches, as I wish to rush to her, knowing our time again together may never come, but I stay among my husband's people and await the commencement of the reading.

By the black suit he wears, and the manner in which he carries himself, it is evident that the speaker is a man of some status. Surrounded by members of the Continental Army, they are as much for protection as for ceremony, for I see many keep a wary eye on those of us who stand apart, and to the woods that surround this place. One man stands out among his troops: I only know him to be Major General Schuyler, as the presence of this distinguished guest's name spreads among all gathered. I listen as our neighbour, Harmonas Cryderman, tells Peter, "It seems he has taken up residence in Sir John's home while he is here. I should say it a great insult to think a family is left without means as a result of this betrayal. It is a sad day that we witness, for all future days are left to God alone to decide our fate." My sisters, too, have overheard, and they, not having been privy to such talk before now, appear alarmed. I smile meekly at them, trying to provide such comfort as may be had by my small gesture.

The great orator, taking his place at the podium, allows his booming voice to proclaim:

"This document having been read in the great cities of our thirteen colonies, I bring to you today great tidings: Freedom and independence are at hand!" A thunderous cheer arises from those gathered tightly together at the foot of the podium. Awaiting the subsiding of this, the great man stands serenely, his serious look unwavering in its expression, utterly focused on the principal task with which he had been charged. "It is my privilege to bring to you now, good folk of Johnstown, on behalf of the Continental Congress, the newly ratified Declaration of Independence."

Unfurling the large broadsheet he carries, he begins:

"In Congress, July 4, 1776.
"The unanimous Declaration of the thirteen united States of America,

"When in the Course of human events, it becomes necessary for one people to dissolve the political bands which have connected them with another, and to assume among the powers of the earth, the separate and equal station to which the Laws of Nature and of Nature's God entitle them, a decent respect to the opinions of mankind requires that they should declare the causes which impel them to the separation."

Each word stings me, as I know with the approval of this document, this "declaration," has settled our fate. With the words: "We must, therefore, acquiesce in the necessity, which denounces our Separation, and hold them, as we hold the rest of mankind, Enemies in War, in Peace Friends" still fixed in my mind, I wonder where we stand. Either we should remain as natural citizens within our own community, or we should leave this place. Either way, we are set upon a new course in this life. In thinking back upon the past seven days and our life of tending to the crops, animals, and household as usual, we realize that over these many days our fate had been sealed; and this day, this reading, was merely the evidence of it.

As the mayhem erupts about us upon completion of the ceremony, we — those who hold true to our loyalty — understand are not welcome at this celebration. Just as we begin our long, silent walk back to our homes, I turn and see my mother and father walking away in the distance. As though I have willed it, my mother turns to me and smiles sadly, and a knowing passes between us, that we shall not look upon one another again in many days to come — if ever.

CHAPTER 7

August 1776

It is a distressing sight that the crops, now ready for harvest, lie in wait of people who are no longer there to tend them. The sight of such abundance going to ruin, whether by nature or rebels, who take of it as they will upon their many passes through our quiet community, reminds me of those who would now be helping one another to bring in the crops. Our people are a people of common purpose, to work as one that none should be superior to the other; this ideal has left with Sir John, and, upon a final accounting, 170 of our neighbours, friends . . . and family.

I pray each morn and night that they have found abundance in the places they have fled to. We have not had word, but my dearest tells me we are to expect none, for he is sure when Sir John returns, it will be to restore his people to our lands; and we remain to safeguard what we can until that time. And when I cannot help but cry for friends and family I no longer see, he reminds me most tenderly that we shall be reunited after all this trouble has passed. However, it is the friends and family that I see but cannot embrace that pains me most. In his flight with so many, we have fallen under watchful eyes, and to gather with those few left would cause concern to our once trusted friends. Our neighbours who seek this "liberty" no longer wave in a genial manner but now look upon us with suspicion.

Sensing a growing desperation among our people, my father-in-law, wise and steady, has called his sons together at our home upon this night, and I am to keep a watchful eye for those who would convict us for rallying to a cause wholly based on our heritage, and not upon the evidence that we had stayed and continued to work as before. Did this not signal hope that we should resolve our differences and come together as one again? This belief, once so sure in my heart, and in the heart of my dearest, falters. It is a strange way to live in places so loved, among people who were once loved, and now . . . are strangers to each other.

In the haze of dusk, I busy myself picking the red, ripened apples from my tree, and as I look to the west for my husband's brothers, who must be ushered into our home unnoticed, I am lost momentarily in the joy of seeing the abundance my tree has produced. I imagine the many delicious desserts that will make a long winter's night meal a delight. As the valley begins its nightly slumber, the crickets that have made the air hum throughout the long, hot day now become quiet and give way to the frogs, whose songs lull us to sleep nightly. With a few fleeting sparks of light through the broad leaves of the forest, the sun dips below the treeline. Just as I strain to look through the mists that begin to form in the hollows, I see our men appear from the cornfield, which towers above their heads. Perhaps they have waited for just this moment to disguise their arrival. They do not talk, but make their way in silent unison to the back door and disappear into the house. I am sure they have seen me, perhaps even watched as I picked my apples, but the serious nature of their meeting has made the usual friendly greetings trivial when such matters are to be discussed.

Gathering the heavy basket, I think about the families now left alone in their homes while ours fills. I should have liked to see my sisters and mother-in-law, for it has been many weeks since we have had occasion to meet. I wonder if they fear as I, for I cannot help but feel this meeting tonight signals a change for us.

Opening the back door to bring in my harvest, the men jump at the sound. "I am sorry—I did not mean to startle you." They look, not composed as my father-in-law, who has not reacted to such an intrusion, but rather anxious. Even my beloved shows his relief in his realization that it is just I. As I struggle with the weight of my basket, the usual pleasant manner of these men reappears, safe within the confines of our home. I cannot prevent a smile as all but my father-in-law make an effort to help. I look toward him, and see he stifles a laugh, as I now do. Seeing Peter's offer of help, the others sit down and become quiet and serious once more. "Let me take those, my dear. You should not be carrying such a heavy basket." I am shocked that he has hinted at my condition in front of the others—and in realizing the same, he simply puts the basket upon the table and turns to rejoin his kin.

We are to welcome a new child in the months to come, a blessing to be sure, but not as it was with my boy, who now sleeps soundly in his cradle; his arrival filled me with a purity of love when I first knew of his time on this earth. It was as though I were transformed in the utmost. I do feel joyful, but this arrival, in such unknown times, makes me fearful about the world that welcomes our child.

Pulling a stool to the table to rest upon, for I already feel the burden of the growing life within, I look out the window into the darkness and think of Lady Johnson this night. As the men talk of the troubles that surround us, and the vigilance we must maintain in our every move to deflect suspicion, it has made me feel vulnerable. I see that Peter, once sure and strong, now seeks the guidance of his father. I do not fault him for it, as we are in times unknown to all, and the wisdom his father has is sought after most ardently.

Peter fears not for himself, but for me and the children. Though he has not expressed such things, for it would be improper, I know it to be true by the way he looks at me, our boy, and upon the child to come. His brothers seek the same surety of the safety of their women-folk and children. It is a hard truth to know we will become such a burden should flight be necessary. These men, sitting sullenly at our table now, have seen the results of women and children left behind, and do not wish this for us. We have many a day bundled food to be transported in secret to these poor unfortunates, so that they might survive.

As I peel the apples, the candle wavers from the soft, cool breezes blowing through the open window. It is a welcome reprieve on the hot days at the end of our growing season. The house retains such oppressive heat, but I do not open the door as usual to welcome the refreshing night air; only the window in front of me welcomes the outside world in. We are sheltered in the safety of our home . . . I pray.

As the hushed conversation continues, I imagine myself in Lady Johnson's stead, and what I would do should the rebels come for me in such a condition. It was perplexing that Sir John had not taken his wife and young children with him in his escape from impending arrest, but within days it became evident why this was so. But a few days after his departure, these ruthless men came back to Johnson Hall to arrest the poor woman, and take her from the comfort of her home. Of course, we are told she protested and made great pleas to stay, as she was with child, and despite her willingness to abandon propriety and disclose her condition, it was to no avail. It was much boasted by the members of our community who align with this rebel cause that great "dignity" was afforded to Lady Johnson, in that she was allowed to travel by carriage to Albany. With her sister Margaret to aid with the children and her needs upon the journey, and exile, the destination did not seem to create pity in the hearts of those who told the stories.

Though I heard tales of Albany and the treatment of people in prisons only from listening to the conversations of my husband's people, it was obvious this fear was ever in their minds. It was evident on these occasions that they did not wish me to hear the details, but in their fervour, it was difficult to contain their anger at such tyranny and injustice. I had heard them say, "Many die before they are brought to trial, and the rest should wish for death to escape the misery of their condition."

"But Father, we have much land that has taken generations to gain. It is not all our neighbours who have been so fortunate. Are we to abandon our hard work and sacrifice?" I instantly listen in, for now they are speaking of the fears I have entertained throughout the night.

"My sons, if we must abandon the land, we must. There may be little choice between land and loved ones. We will return after the troubles have ceased to reclaim what is rightfully ours."

"Father, what if this does not come to pass? What if we do not return, and the liberty these rebels seek prevails?"

"Then, my sons, we will start anew in the king's lands." His voice left no doubt that there was but one choice if it needed to be made.

Looking around at the home we had built and started our family in, I dread the thought that it might be lost to us if the troubles do not subside.

Thinking of Lady Johnson once more, now heavy with child, I wonder how she fares. I pray she is spared some comfort for her status. Surely this would not be so for those who work the lands, as ourselves. One could not imagine the horror of being arrested in such a state. I have never had to think on such things, but now, forced to face the possibility, I feel a steadfastness in protecting my children — born and yet to be. It is strange and unknown to me, for I could ever rely on my beloved for our protection. I imagine in this way, as a wife and mother, Lady Johnson would have relied on Sir John. But alone, and at the mercy of men full with ambitions that will not be quenched with any form of negotiation on the matters of "liberty," appealing to common decency is of no use. It is a vile reflection of men's hearts that this should be so.

Unable to suppress the bitterness rising in me, I think of our home, set in a valley full of women and children, or those too aged or infirm, left upon their homesteads. The fortunate had some family left to care for them; the ill-fated . . . I cannot bear this thought in my current state. Should I be left? Arrested as poor Lady Johnson? Becoming lightheaded, I realize I must suppress such thoughts or I should become a burden as the men speak of important matters.

I breathe in the cool air to come to my senses and, turning back to my work, I peel the apples, a simple pleasure I shall not take for granted.

CHAPTER 8

August 6, 1777

It storms today, the rain falling heavy upon our crops, and Peter watches out the window praying that God should spare our wheat to bring us through winter. It has been many a day since we have experienced storms such as this, and the force of them leaves Peter feeling forlorn. Where once we would have been assured of abundance with the sharing among our community, now, with so few, it is imperative that our crop alone should yield what we require to survive.

Soaked thoroughly, Philip, my husband's youngest brother, appears from the field. His news must be urgent indeed to brave such weather. Peter knows this, for his face reflects great concern, and opening the door to allow Philip to pass, he does not extend his usual greeting, but abruptly inquires, "What news, brother?"

Standing no farther than he must inside the door, obviously not wanting to create a puddle on the floor, Philip looks at the water that spreads about his feet; it is plain he cannot prevent this. He looks as though his mood matches his bedraggled appearance. "Father gathers us, Peter, for there is news to tell that changes all."

I pretend not to listen, as always, and run to fetch a cloth for Philip to dry his sopping hair. "Catrina, please bring some of my clothing so that my brother might have the comfort of dry clothing while we wait for the others." I do as instructed and soon return.

"Thank you, Catrina. I am sorry to cause such grief."

"It is none you cause, dear brother; you are always welcome. May I offer you some water?"

"No, I shall sit at the table and await Father's arrival." Philip is the most quiet and withdrawn of all the Eamer men, and while some may say it is his young age that makes this so, for he is not yet seventeen, I sense he is of a gentle heart and has been much affected by these times of trouble we experience.

Soon, hearing the sounds of many hooves galloping up to our door, I realize more than just our kin arrive. As Peter opens the door, he watches as the horses are hidden in our barns so that their presence might not reveal this gathering. Men quickly make their way through the open door and each takes a seat at the table. With three additional visitors to our home to discuss a matter of grave importance, this is not the usual distress we face. I hurry to the summer kitchen, where I can seem to busy myself with preserving, but will have the advantage of satisfying my curiosity.

Mathias plays quietly in his room, while our baby Ruby sleeps soundly in the basket at my feet. Briefly looking down at her, I marvel at such softness in her features. She is a quiet child, rarely requiring more than to be fed and clothed, and so I do not fear her interruption of my listening to what transpires. Dear Lord, forgive me, for I know this is most wicked but I sense this conversation will affect us most profoundly. Glancing at Ruby again, I feel the all-too-familiar pang of fear.

"The news is grim?" My father-in-law, who, I had noticed, was pale and gaunt upon his entry, seems to be drained of his usual assured disposition.

"I am afraid it is," says Isaac Mattice, one of our visitors whom I have not seen these many months and is markedly changed, for he has the look of a man much older than his years. "Just this morning, Sir John and Captain Butler have joined with General St. Leger of the king's forces at Oriska and stopped the advancement of the rebels upon Fort Stanwix — or, as the rebels have come to know it, Fort Schuyler."

On hearing the name, I reflect back on a day not but a year ago when we saw the man this fort has now been named after. As he had stood in uniform behind the man who read the Declaration to us, I remember thinking him a fearful presence, for he surely meant to rid these lands of our people. His disposition seemed arrogant, and I remember feeling disdain for him, praying God would forgive my un-Christian thoughts. It was plain from his expression, on the occasions in which he glanced in our direction, that he thought the same of us. With the naming of a fort in his honour, it signalled he must have been having some success in promoting the rebel cause and the sentiment expressed so profoundly in the Declaration read on that day.

"Is this where the men of our community mustered to only a few days ago?" Martin seems to have had a realization that is most distressing to him. His usual stoicism is gone, and I wonder what torments him so.

"Yes. The militia were to meet at Fort Schuyler and provide aid in its defence from His Majesty's loyal forces."

"I pray, even as we disagree, we will see many come back, for there is many a homestead with no man to tend to his coming harvest and family."

I hear Martin's voice falter. I had heard them speak of the great numbers of men who had left, but in their caution, these men who had departed to join Herkimer had kept their destination quiet, as they believe us to be spies, and as such, even their families were not privy to such news. Many of these men now consisted of our own people who once sought to remain neutral as we had, but had chosen to align themselves with the rebels, believing it the only way to safeguard their place in these lands. This situation is dire in its confusion. Militia and armies meeting upon the battlefield were but neighbours, friends, and family only weeks, months — and I suddenly realize now — years before. They, who defended this fort, defended it from their own. The gravity of the situation came to bear.

My father-in-law, having taken up the role of leader of this group, bids, "Please, Isaac, tell us what you know."

As Isaac gathers his thoughts, it is obvious he is much grieved by the implication of his message. "My brother, Henry, whom you know to have left with Sir John two years ago, has met with me just this hour to send word of what has transpired. Having the blessing of Sir John to do so, he now returns as we speak to rejoin his regiment."

Beginning the wretched story, he does not delay in its most grisly detail, "It is said, the creek ran red with the blood of so many men; such wretched ways to die as they have seen." It is noticeable that this man, usually so composed, struggles with the news that lays heavy upon his heart. "No thoughts to the rules of war were given; a most vicious and chaotic attack ensued. General Herkimer, accused of sympathies to our cause, for as you know his own brother fights with General St. Leger, having had his good senses riled from him, gave the command that they should circumvent their orders to wait until aid was requested and instead made his way to remove His Majesty's forces from their position. Their General Herkimer paid dearly for his zeal, for he died, his horse shot dead from under him, and he wounded most grievously in the leg."

As I listen, I realize that these many months, as trouble has stirred, the hearts of men seem to have darkened and their hatred grown. I fret, thinking this may be an evil force that sweeps over our good nature and pits us one against the other; and surely God will have no forgiveness for such sin. I pray silently now as I continue to listen.

"Having been sent word by Molly Brant, once of this place, that General Herkimer was beginning his march, General St. Leger sent our forces, including those under Sir John's and Captain Butler's command, along with militia and Indian allies under the command of the great Mohawk Joseph Brant, to assemble and lie in wait in the dark of the forest to set upon them as they entered the ravine, along the creek bed. As the rebel militia, and their Indian allies, entered this place, our men descended upon them before they could reach their destination. Much of the fighting was done in such close proximity that hand-to-hand combat was a brutal necessity. With such unbridled viciousness—" Isaac suddenly stops. "I shall not burden you, my friends, with what I have heard from my brother's own lips. It is as I should never have hoped to know of men; that they should be capable of such evil." Isaac's voice trails off. It is obvious he chokes back tears of grief and rage mixed as one. I am glad he goes no further with his description, for already I am beset with terror.

Gathering himself again, he continues, "As they fought, our camps established outside the fort, were set upon with three-pound guns and weapons as were at the ready from the fort. Charging at our position, our forces were scattered into the woods, the camps destroyed, and much of our intelligence captured, making our forces remaining in the valley precarious. Sir John has taken position in a secret location and will assemble with Captain Butler and General St. Leger upon this night. Joseph Brant has taken his men to pursue the rebels who fled the field and he is expected to rejoin our forces once his work is done."

This "work" leaves me feeling ill, and the men in stunned silence, for not a sound comes from the room. Had I not heard this solitary voice telling of such things, I should think my home vacant.

"The great Iroquois alliance has been shattered, and our enemies grow as such. We must be ever-more vigilant as we work in our fields, and upon the night, keep a wary eye to the dark, for treachery seeks out retribution for this success of our forces. Hundreds yet lie dead upon the floor of the ravine, most from the militia that gathered at Herkimer's calling. We shall not see many return to our community, and this surely signals destitution for their families. Were it not for sentiments toward us, and I suspect further hatred for our plight, we should care for them as we do our own womenfolk left behind. But as it is, we are ordered not to provide aid to the enemy, in any form."

"Does Sir John come for us?" Our neighbour, Jacob Silmser, an elder in our community, who was left behind when Sir John first fled, inquires with a hope that makes the response pitiful.

"No, not this time, dear sir. There is much work to be done before we may leave this place."

My father-in-law, who addresses Mr. Silmser now, is aware, as we all are, that because of infirmity, he, only making it to this table for discussion because his son Nicholas stayed behind to care for him and brings him this day by buckboard, will not be seeing the king's lands of Quebec. It is widely admired that Nicholas should keep his wife and children in these troubled lands, when they had much to gain by leaving. They had not acquired land as our kin, but instead remained because of loyalties to their people, this place, and his aged, widower father.

"And what of Quebec: is it as foretold? Does the king provide for our needs in this new land?" It is obvious from his optimism and lack of understanding of what has been conveyed, that the poor Mr. Silmser is spared the knowledge of his reality, for he is surely unaware that he will not be taken when the time comes. "It is," Isaac says in a sympathetic tone.

Turning again to his dire task, Isaac warns, "I tell you this now, my friends: If we stay in this valley, we do so knowing our lives are in danger, for reprisal shall swiftly follow. Sir John sends word that he has not forsaken us, and will call upon us to aid in our people's restoration, and should this not come to pass, will send for our people to bring us to the safety that awaits us in Quebec." This message is ominous, for Sir John now makes mention of our removal, that our righteous course may not be rewarded.

"Isaac, we understand what you tell us now, and I pray that our Lord shall see us through this time to once again live in peace among our neighbours." This battle, so ruthless in that it tears friends and families apart, takes its toll on my father-in-law's resolve. His voice does not have the confidence it has had in many a discussion around this table before. "Take heed, dear friends. I wish you well, and pray we may gather again in happier times."

I hear Isaac rise, as do the others. With sombre wishes for safety upon the journey home, the house is still once more, with only Peter looking out the window as his father and brothers disappear around the bend upon their horses, Philip astride with his father. With the sun making its presence known once more, the dark clouds dissipate, and we are left, not rejoicing in its return and salvation of our crops, but rather with heavy hearts that our days are surely coming to an end in this place. Hope fades with such news.

Looking out my window to the moon that casts a silvery glow on me, I lie in our bed crying quietly so as to not cause further distress to my beloved, who lies close by, his warmth and the rise and fall of his chest making me feel less alone, though he sleeps. I suffer most miserably, for I should not have heard such things as today, and once having been glad to understand more than my sisters, I now envy their innocence. I do not understand the ways of men, for how can brother fight brother in such brutal ways? Knowing the creek ran red with blood — and done so at the hands of loved ones, was too much to bear. I keep my eyes fixed upon the moon, for when I shut them I see red, and cannot rid my mind of faces I have known and loved.

CHAPTER 9

Christmas 1779

I watch our three children receive their gifts this day, a day we would once have celebrated with kin, but now do so alone in secret celebration. Mathias is glad to have a new shirt, much like his father's, for he so wishes to be like him. Already he is so in manner and grows into a fine and dutiful son. He has learned much about tending the animals and helps to plan the crops we will sow upon the spring, though this is much changed in these two years.

Our Jacob, born these fifteen months, pulls at the blanket I have knitted for him. In our isolation from kin, and the loneliness this brings about, its making occupied many a day and night, and I pray the small pleasure it brought me does the same for this little one. As he ambles about, I am well pleased that he is robust and healthy. Born into such times of want, it is a miracle that my children thrive.

Ruby sits near the fire, caressing the doll I have made her of old scraps of cloth. Though it is small, for little in this house has not come to some useful employ, it nevertheless brings purpose back to my quiet one. She simply calls it "Dolly," and no amount of persuasion will have her call it anything but. Rocking to and fro, she sings the songs I so oft sing to her. She has needed much comfort these many days, for she is wise and knows we suffer. Our altered state has made her pensive and unsure, and when she retreats, I pull her to me and sing softly—as my mother did the last time I saw her upon the gathering at Johnson Hall. Though I am a married woman, I often think about her comfort and wish to see her again. To know she has not yet met our Ruby or Jacob leaves me inconsolable. Many a night I cry myself to sleep thinking of her, for I should dearly love to see her and tell her of my fears, for they are many. I have heard news from our rare visitor, Isaac, that they struggle as we do, but are well and have not yet left the valley.

With little to prepare for dinner, I set the broth to warm over the fire and turn, smiling, to Ruby, hoping to receive the same in return. I am pleased when I do. We shall not have a goose, as other Christmases, for we celebrate alone. And so, with our meagre meal warming, I set myself upon my chair to mend some of Peter's clothing. Staring back into the glowing fire, I reflect on our existence and cannot find much joy in it, even on this, the day of our Lord's birth. Our kin were right to fear those many months ago; for Oriska changed our life in the valley.

Much of what was predicted has come to pass. We have been held to account for the disaster at Oriska, and the many more battles within our valley. That the rebels can visit no retribution on Sir John and his men after the battles are fought, the wounded carried off, and the dead buried, they have ensured they make us suffer in his stead. Our harvest has been much diminished by the Continental Army, which plunders it as they will to feed their men or destroys it if they have no means of transporting it. Though we managed to protect enough to see us through that first winter after Oriska, we very nearly starved and found ourselves eating what little we could find on the land when spring came. We did not want to slaughter our animals, for we knew once they were gone, we would not be able to sustain ourselves on the land. It was only through the intercession of our neighbour Robert Wall, a respected member of the Committee of Safety, who knew we had not taken up arms against our own people, that our animals were spared. Our crops had already been burned when he arrived, but a small allotment was spared, and this is what we subsisted on for many a sorrowful day. Once a valley of plenty, we now know not to cultivate crops as we once did, for they will surely be taken or destroyed, and so this winter passes with my vigilance as to how much we may eat daily to bring us through late spring, when early crops might again provide for us.

Winter is bleak, much as our hope. We pray together within the solitary confines of our home, which has come to feel as a fortress amongst enemies. I despair in our situation, and this I know is a sin, for many families in our valley, whether they be our own people, or those seeking liberty, are all suffering equally. Many have no one coming for them—for hundreds were lost at Oriska—no one looking to their future needs, and they are left most desperately at the mercies of life. I pray this liberty they so ardently seek does not see them left destitute and starving—though we have heard tell of such things.

The broth boils, and as I set the bread and butter upon the table, the children gather, and Peter looks over the commotion as everyone prepares for our meagre but sustaining meal. He is melancholy today; he, too, feels the burden of isolation. Though we are together, we are separated from our people and our church and we feel as though we exist in a desolate landscape at the edge of the world. Holding hands around the table, we bow our heads. "We are grateful, dear Lord, for your mercy upon us. The bounty before us is only by your generous hand, and on this, your son's day of birth, we thank you most humbly for your many blessings. Amen."

Our prayers at mealtime have become short, as all are eager to fill hungry bodies with much-needed sustenance; we eat only what we must to get from meal to meal, day to day. Jacob often cries for more, and being the youngest, we often cannot refuse. Peter will not see us give of ours; he is thin with the many morsels he has shared. He takes delight in Jacob's healthy constitution, and so I will not deny him this one pleasure.

Hastily setting the candle on the table, the house is cold, and I rush to enter the warmth of our bed. I look forward to sleep, for it provides such a wonderful reprieve, when it comes; but too many a long, lonely night have I lain awake praying for salvation. The separation from the life I knew haunts me this night, and I worry it should not bring the rest I need—the reprieve I seek. Waiting for Peter to join me, I watch as my breath meets the air, forming a willowy, white mist that floats about before disappearing entirely. As the candle flickers, it casts shadows that dance about the room, creating an element of entertainment that captures my imagination, and I frolic with the creatures I imagine these to be, much as I had done in my childhood. "Catrina? Catrina?"

I startle to find Peter looking at me, perplexed. "What do you see?"

I laugh. "Fairies; just fairies."

He frowns, but mimics my teasing, and says, "Oh, the fairies are back, are they? I shall have to chase them away in the morning." He lifts the blanket, allowing a cold rush of air to enter what is just warming, and I retreat with the shock of it. He comes close and beckons me to lay my head upon his warm chest. I lean to blow out the candle and nestle into him, Safe for the moment, I feel myself moving into the abyss of sleep.

CHAPTER 10

May 16, 1780

I sense the life growing within me, previously signalling the beginning of new and exciting times in our home, but with all the trouble of the revolution — which it now most certainly and decidedly is — I do not want to burden Peter with the news. I will wait until times are more settled. The spring, which generally brings a sense of renewed hope, now, nearly a full four years from the signing of the Declaration, holds no promise that there will be a way of going forward and emerging as one community. The hoped-for resolution is not to be. Not even the early buds of my beautiful tree — nor the life I hold within me — brings any sense of hope for a future here. As I return to kneading the dough, I am startled from my thoughts.

"We have been called before the Committee. I shall return before dark." Peter swiftly exits the house, and I am left with nothing but silence and the confused looks of my three little ones playing upon the floor.

The sudden and loud BANG! of the door and the angered voices entering send the children scurrying to my side. Though these are men they hold dear, their demeanour is foreboding and . . . desperate.

"Catrina, take them upstairs." His unfamiliar manner strikes a sense of fear within me. This man, whom I love and know to be kind, is now distant and a stranger to me.

Setting the children to quietly play in their room, I leave them to go to my own room, where I can overhear some of what is being said.

I cannot return to my work in the kitchen without raising suspicion about my intent, so finding refuge in the corner of my room, which is directly above them, I listen. It must be the result of having been called before the Committee, as they have returned unusually early, they having left but an hour before. In that it takes at least twenty minutes to ride to the Van Alstyne house, their speedy return signals that something is amiss — and terribly so.

"That we should be called as though we were not neighbours to those who stand in judgment of us and call into question our motives, our allegiances . . . that our religious convictions and high moral standing in this community should not matter is deplorable!" I have never heard my father-in-law raise his voice in such volume before, and the harshness with which he speaks his words might have at one time seemed foreign, but is now familiar. My Peter, too, has the same voice — the same cold, hardened voice. These gentle men, who love their land and their people so — who have worked hard to show their thankfulness for a debt they owed to our king — are now changed; though I pray not irreparably so. But this, as everything else in our world, is not assured.

"Father, what are we to do, not for ourselves, but for our families? How are we to continue to live side by side with those who would call us enemy as quickly as they had once called us friend?" It is obvious from Peter's voice that he is completely unsure of their course of action. I hear the same desperate yearning often heard in the voices of my little ones. My Peter, a husband and father, is beseeching his beloved father's sage advice — who in turn remains silent.

An urgent banging at the door makes one of the men jump, slamming the chair to the floor in a large crash that sends me to reassure the children who have run to my door. I set them all upon my bed under the blanket and tell them to pray silently as I continue to listen.

"No one must know of my presence. My father will have no mercy on any man who goes against the Whig cause, regardless of who that man might be to him." Though the underlying tone in his voice spoke of regret, the clear and most evident was that tinged with a deep, brewing anger. "My uncle rides tonight to meet Sir John and join the cause. I, too, shall ride as soon as I have made a few stops prior to my departure."

"Pray, Master Ball, will you not sit and tell us your message?"

"No, sir, I shall not rest, for I come to warn you now, good friends — you must not delay — leave in haste upon nightfall, for they will come for you this night."

"And if we stay? What then?" My father-in-law seems to only half-heartedly make a gesture of standing firm, for I suspect he understands, as we all now do, that there are no options left.

"Dear Mr. Eamer, I have warned many, but regretfully not all were at their homes to receive warning: Prior to the call to stand before the Committee, many of our neighbours were being rounded up, charged as spies against the rebel cause, and sent to Albany." I could hear the resignation in his voice. He had much to lose by coming to warn us, and in this gesture I took hope that all goodness in the world was not lost.

"Albany." I hear the "thud" as my father-in-law sits upon his chair, completely and utterly defeated. I do not need to be in the room to get a full sense of what their faces look like; they all look at each other in stunned silence. Finally, one of the men addresses the group, though so softly I cannot recognize the speaker, "and what of their families?"

"Many are left behind to fend for themselves. The orders are being given that none should be helped that do not support the Whig cause. I am sorry that I cannot stay to provide more details, my friends, but I must away. Uncle waits upon the hillside only until dark and then makes his way to Sir John."

"Yes, yes, of course. Please give your uncle our wishes for a safe journey. And we owe you a debt of gratitude for your warning." I hear the chairs screech upon the floor, as the men rise to say goodbye to young Master Ball. In turn, my husband and his brothers thank him and wish him a good and safe journey.

"Do not delay, my friends, for the outcome is decisive." The door slams. Silence.

Then the men begin to speak in hurried, yet hushed tones, devising a plan. Though I try and listen, my mind is filled with the fate of those already on their way to the prisons in Albany, which we have heard to be the most inhumane places — "cold, dark, and decrepit," these having been described by those who had loved ones taken. I worry that our men could suffer the same fate and wonder if my father and brothers are among those already taken . . . if my mother and sisters have been left to fend for their families alone . . . if I, too, will be among these unfortunates. It seems that neutrality, as our religious convictions demand, is not an option anymore. If one does not choose a side, then we are put in the position of enemy.

I am lost in my own thoughts. Peter enters the room and announces, "We have been marked as traitors."

CHAPTER 11

May 16, 1780

"Shall I prepare the children, Peter?" I inquire with such desperation that I am surprised I contain the scream that wells in me. My mind goes to what we will need upon the journey: blankets, food, water, clothing . . .

"My dear . . . my dearest." Peter's voice is soft again, and I regain a sense of the room I am standing in: my room, with three little ones looking upon me with fear in their eyes at my outburst. Holding both my hands in his own, my beloved looks down at me, his blue-grey eyes shimmering as the tears catch the final light of day in them, "You are not coming." I slump to the floor, unable to stand; all life feels as though it has left me in this moment, and I am helpless. "Mathias, please take the children into your room so that I might console your mother."

My boy, ever-obedient, guides Ruby to their room as he gathers his struggling little brother in his arms.

Left upon the floor, light blinding me as it streams into our bedchamber window, I feel as though I must be in another place and cannot understand what is happening. All I can see is the light and hear only the heart that beats forcefully within my breast. Peter is shaking me most violently, and I begin to hear his voice again. "Catrina. Catrina. You must listen, now, for our time together draws to a close." His voice is pleading, and though I want to help ease his pain, I am lost in my own despair. "I will come for you and the children once we have found Sir John and receive instruction on how we might safeguard your passage. It is a fearsome route to Quebec, my dear, and I fear we are ill-advised to leave as one."

"But, Peter, what will become of us left here with no form of protection? These people who call us enemy — traitors — shall surely come for us, and what then? Will they take us away to Albany just as our own poor folk, as poor Lady Johnson? I cannot bear it, Peter. I CANNOT!" I am surprised to be so disobedient, for I have never been so before. I ache to tell him why I fear I am incapable of defending our children, but I do not, for it is plainly evident he is as desperate as I. We have been set onto a fateful path with few options. "Peter, I do not know what to do."

"Nor do I." He breaks down and we hold each other in a most desperate embrace. Each holding onto the other, we are but lost children, looking desperately to the other for salvation and being able to provide none. Placing my head on his chest, I am glad to feel his arms around me, safe and warm, if only for a moment. "I love you." His gentleness returns, and my beloved, the man who has been my husband these five years, has come back to me. The world that has taken so much from us has now left us with only this to cling to. Our love will have to be the strength on which we rely to survive this ordeal.

"I love you, Peter."

Tears are of little use to us now and, as we gather ourselves, we embrace one last time before he rises and reaches his hand to aid me from the floor. I am glad our inelegant embrace has not revealed that which would surely burden him further.

Now resuming his serious manner, he continues with the directions he must convey before his departure. "I shall have to give the illusion that all is as usual, but I will need you to prepare a few supplies for my journey."

"Yes, of course." I hesitate, not wanting to know the answer . . . "When do you depart?"

"When the dark of night provides disguise, I ride to meet Father and my brothers, but it must be before the moon rises."

As I gaze at the late evening sky, the sun now set for another day, I know the time draws near. "Shall I make you a meal to shore you up for the ride?"

"No, I must tend to the animals. I will provide additional feed to allow you time to prepare the children in the morning, and, though young, our Mathias knows much of what must be done in this regard." I hear the pride he takes in having taught our son the love of the land, and how to care for the animals that aid in the everyday working of our farm. It is as it had been when he was but a boy, and his father had imparted the same lessons. To think this time is coming to an abrupt end for our Mathias, only four, is something I cannot imagine I will find the words to help him understand. For a boy to have no father would cost him dearly in this life. I fervently pray that their time together should come to pass again.

"If it must be done, slaughter the animals lest the Continental Army or our neighbours take them for their own needs. They have taken our liberty to live as we wish, and we shall not provide for their needs, even if they attempt to take things by force. We shall be the masters of the animals we keep, and for our own needs; and by our hands will they die if need be." This man who stands before me, shaking with such gripping anger in his voice as I have never heard, is much changed already. In being forced to abandon his family, the land he loved, and his liberty, he now sacrifices the forgiving nature that has seen him through these many years of injustice. But it seems that at last there is a limit to his ability to forgive.

As he opens the door to go to the barns for the last time, I inquire as to the others being left behind as well. "And your mother and sisters: who cares for them? Shall I go to them to offer aid?"

"No! You must act as usual; you will be watched closely. Do not give them reason to suspect you of collusion." These strangers — "them" — are people I once knew.

The dark of night, having come all too soon, signals that the life I have known comes to an end. Peter hastily enters the back door, announcing, "I must leave at once. My father and brothers wait for me." I hand him the bundle I have prepared. The food supplies are spare, as we have had to make do with little of late, having nearly finished the last of our winter provisions. Handing him a warm woollen blanket from our bed, he immediately hands it back, saying, "Keep it, for you may have need of it, should I not send for you as quickly as I hope." His lack of surety in coming for us before winter has made the full weight of my responsibility come to bear; and yet, with no choice, I must remain resolute in my efforts.

"Please come as soon as you may, but stay safe, my dear, for we have no place in this world without you." I look at him, and though tears cover my face, I show him the strength I command in his stead. "Will you say goodbye to the children?" His lip quivers with the thought. His eyes are red, evidence of his struggle when thinking on all that is taking place. His time alone in the barn, I suspect, was spent in quiet prayer and reflection on a most insurmountable task—to tear himself away from his family, leaving us to the mercies of an unknown world. I pity him, for I know this will wound him deeply. I do not follow him up the stairs, for I cannot bring myself to stand by and watch the faces of our children in saying goodbye to their father. Perhaps the Lord would spare our youngest any knowledge of what was happening because of his tender age, and even Ruby might not comprehend such things, but Mathias, our bright boy, will comprehend what his father's departure means.

Through the floorboards, I hear his deep, rich voice speaking to them in gentle, affectionate ways. No sound comes from the children in response, but they will heed their father's words. Peter descends the stairs, and just as I approach for one last embrace, Mathias rushes down the stairs and holds his father's leg in a frantic grip. In contrast to Peter's stature, and by the tears streaming down his rounded, flushed cheeks, Mathias, usually stoic and proud in reverence for his father, shows his true age. I pick him up, pulling hard to release him, but in doing so, he yells out in a desperate, heart-wrenching cry, "Papa! Papa! Don't go."

Struggling to control Mathias from leaping from my arms to grab what cannot be had, Peter reaches for his pack with one hand, and grabs me by the shoulder with the other, whispering to me most desperately, "I feel I ask too much of you, my dear. I pray I shall look upon your face and those of our children again." With that, he immediately exits the house, mounts his horse, and disappears into the dark to meet his father and brothers.

Soon, even the evidence of hooves upon the trail disappear, and I stand holding my bewildered son with only the sound of the trees rustling in the wind, and the frogs that once lulled us into our slumber, continuing as always . . . as though nothing has changed.

CHAPTER 12

May 17, 1780

I lay awake through the night after Peter's hasty departure to meet Sir John. Though I had not heard the details through the floorboards, Peter soon told me all that had been planned, and tried to impart some warnings of what I might come to expect when the discovery of their departure came to light. I endeavoured to listen, committing his words to memory, though I could only focus on the rich tenor of his voice, and the desperation of my most beloved concerned only for my well-being and that of his little ones. The details of his sorrowful eyes, golden hair, and the smell of his salty sweat, swirled about, clouding my ability to hear what he was saying. I wanted to get lost in his essence — to be sheltered in our home, safe from a world gone astray. When upon leaving he kissed my forehead, his warm lips leaving a lasting mark, my hopes for all that we had planned, all that I had wished for, left with him. And now, lying in our bed, little ones breathing soft and steady, having cried themselves to sleep, I am alone, unable to cry, unable to fear; simply lost in my last moments with him.

As the quarter moon comes into view of my window, casting soft, dim light on little fair-haired heads — one, two, three, the sounds of angry voices grow in the darkness, just as predicted.

BANG, BANG, BANG.

I do not want to move. I am scared.

BANG, BANG, BANG.

"Peter Eamer, you are being called for questioning. Make yourself known." The voice, while foreboding, was strangely familiar. "One more warning, Peter, and then we shall come in to get you forcibly."

Pulling the wool blanket from the chair, I wrap it around my shoulders and run down the stairs with no shoes upon my feet. The floor is jarring—as cold as ice, for Peter had told me to let the fire go out tonight. As I take my final step to the door, the pounding sounds as though someone is battering a tree against it. I am sure it will shatter, but miraculously it is holding. I open it, jumping back to avoid the offending object. Instantly men pour into my home, uninvited, unwelcome.

"Peter Eamer, show yourself!"

I stare directly up into the face of Elijah Ball, the very brother of the young man who, just this afternoon, came to warn us of impending danger. Oddly, in this moment, all fear leaves me and suddenly I am filled with rage—and strength.

"He is gone."

"Gone where?" Elijah's eyes are cold with anger and just a hint of . . . grief. "He is gone!" He turns, telling the men the news and seems to instinctively know that searching our home will be of little purpose. Just as abruptly as they had poured in, the men vanish from the house. Elijah pauses for a moment, glaring at me with disdain, and then suddenly slams the door shut behind him. I sense he holds me responsible for the ruin that has befallen his own family. Hearing the children crying upstairs, I make my way up quickly to reassure them. Crawling into bed, I wrap my arms around all three and sing in a loud voice the songs that are familiar and comforting to them and are yet familiar and comforting to me as well in this confusing, altered circumstance.

I hear them yelling, "They have fled!" and though I had not seen the gathered crowd, I believe they are significant in number, judging from the repetition of the message making its way from man to man. "They have fled." They must all have made it out under the darkness of night. I am briefly relieved by this, but know it is just the first step in a treacherous journey to the British colony in the North and Sir John.

Continuing to sing, I pull the little ones ever closer as the barn doors swing open, hitting the sides hard, making the animals inside call out in surprise. The voices of the men are muffled; they are in the barn. These voices, familiar and once friendly, are now changed with anger; no more can I recognize them. I sense the same anger rising within me, for the very survival of my most precious ones is at stake. Already at the mercies of such evil, the poor unfortunate creatures within the walls of the barn will soon meet their fate in a most painful way; but it is the little ones gathered near and my beloved in the chilled, dark night riding to meet Sir John, that I think of. As the first flashes of light begin to show through the boards of the barn, I hear the panicked sounds of the cows and horses. The cries become more frantic, as the flames and smoke begin to escape through the slits in the walls, and the children, having quietly looked upon me as I sang, begin to stir, gazing to the window and the cause of such sounds. My singing cannot drown them out. I hear the barn doors slam shut and the voices of the men hooting and hollering as they fade into the distance, leaving their mark behind.

As the flames grow, the echo of mooing and neighing turns to a screaming, almost human in its call for mercy, it is unbearable to think of the suffering of our poor animals, which had so faithfully tilled the fields and provided our sustenance, asking only to be fed and cared for. My beloved was gentle with them, as he saw them as creatures of God, not simply the means of our livelihood. And now, in their way, they are crying out for salvation. The children are fearful of what they hear, but as they cannot recognize the unfamiliar sounds of the animals perishing in the flames, as such, I explain it is but men having some merriment, for I cannot find a reasonable alternative. "Your father has gone with your grandfather and uncles to find Sir John and he will surely come back to us soon." They seem distracted by the "adventure" story I am making up, but ever the while all I hear are the sounds. Though the tears well, I will not betray my true feelings, for fear it should alarm and frighten those young enough to be sheltered from this horror.

"Mama, is Papa cold outside?" I see that my oldest boy, but a babe of four years, has understood too much already.

The screams do not last long, as the hay is soon aflame and the entire barn engulfed. With flames shooting skyward above the peaks, the flickering light within my room dances about as a ghastly reminder of what I am trying to push to the back of my mind. Yet, while the choking smoke, flames illuminating the room as though day, and heat penetrating our walls are menacing, in that the house could catch fire, it also brings silence. "Sleep, now, for morning comes soon." I pull them closer still, and try to ease the sobbing that consumes them. "Shhh, shhh. We are safe in God's care, my little ones. Mama is here. Mama is here." They look to me again, and I feign surety of our safety with a feeble smile. Lying upon me, they begin to calm. My uncompromising will to protect my precious ones overcomes me, yet even in this, I am not certain I can safeguard them.

Singing once more to lull them into the ease brought by sleep, my little ones soon rest, but I do not. Left with the crackling sounds of the wood that is slowly being consumed, all I see is Peter's frantic, anxious face—not at the thought of his own possible peril, but of mine and the children's. I lay my hand upon one, who now twists and turns, and I continue singing silently to calm my hope for a new beginning, glad that I have some company on a night that is unmercifully long and lonely.

CHAPTER 13

May 17, 1780

As the first light of day turns the night sky into a shade of deep blue, knowing that the day begins anew provides some relief. Assured they are yet peacefully asleep, I ease out of bed slowly and without sound. The house is much too cold, and I must start the fire again. But first, I want to look upon the scar left by the night.

Opening the door, I cannot yet look upon the ruins, and look instead toward the field glistening with a frost set upon the land. It sparkles with the rising sun. The sky is orange and rose, as on so many mornings in a time before, and yet I am unable to reconcile my present circumstance as being part of the same existence. The field where my beloved routinely tread in the early day, is now empty. Though the birds sing, and the geese fly above as always, much life has left this place—a spirit extinguished.

I hesitate to look upon it, but know I must and so gather what strength I possess, exhaustion and ill feeling taking a toll. In a heap of smouldering hay and blackened boards, the retribution for my beloved's flight is complete.

Turning to enter the house, my tree, blooming with the welcome of a new day, reminds me of "before."

# CHAPTER 14

May 19, 1780

May 18, 1780

My Dearest Catrina:

We are but a day away, my dear, yet I feel as though we have crossed into a new world. Our way was made expedient by the waiting sentries upon our journey. Young Master Ball and his uncle had given Sir John word that the warnings had been delivered and to wait for us upon the trails.

And now, my dear, I am imparting a warning to you. This is most serious. Sir John will be leading us back to our homes to retrieve our families in but two nights. I think once you receive this warning, it shall be much sooner, I am afraid. I pray this reaches you before our arrival. Do not rejoice, however, my dear, for it is the intent to lay waste the land as we move. We hear the Continental Army and the rebels are moving from town to town, farm to farm, helping themselves as they will to food stores, leaving families to starve through the harsh winter months. We will not see Washington's army fed while our children starve. It is the only method by which to ensure that all we have worked for will not aid those who have so unjustly judged us.

I think I shall not see you upon our arrival, but there will be warning given, and you must heed this most immediately. The diversion of our efforts to bring retribution upon our town and the valley will provide the disguise for your escape. Pray, my dear wife, for the time is at hand that we must abandon our dream and make way for a new life under the King's protection. Take upon yourself the weapon I had once shown you how to use when our troubles began, for though it had been my hope that you should never require its security, now you must rely upon it. My dear, this journey will be fraught with danger, and I do not ask this of you with a light heart. I know you will find the strength, good wife, to do what must be done.

Please find the few shillings enclosed to use to provide for safe passage on your long and arduous journey. Whatever may happen, you must make your way to Quebec, where there are those who support our noble cause and who will direct you to me.

I go to sleep now praying that you and our precious ones will find the strength to journey to safety. Be assured, my dear, though you must leave our home, we will make a new future under the protection of our King, and, with God's help, we shall plant the seed for generations of our children to come.

Your Ever-Faithful and Loving Husband,
Peter

Silently standing near me as I read the letter, young Hezekiah Alguire looks unsure at me. Knowing he has more news to deliver, I do not delay the inevitable.

"There is more."

"Yes, I am sorry to say."

"Tell me, then. I am quite strong enough." I attempt a smile, to reassure him, for he looks dreadfully apprehensive. A boy of only twelve years, this task seems a great burden for one so young, but I can see in his eyes that he has been witness to much in these few days—as we all have.

"I am to report that your father, Mr. Michael Gallinger, is taken to Albany. Your mother follows to provide comfort as she is able." I struggle to maintain my composure. As my vision dims and I succumb to the shock of such dreadful news, Hezekiah gently guides me to rest upon the doorway, seeming unsure of what more to do. I grab his hand and implore, "And what of the ones left at home?" It is their survival, not their distress, I inquire after. Our much-altered circumstance now requires planning and preparation, leaving little place for mourning.

"They are in the care of the oldest yet at home, Anna, who receives the message you, too, have received. They are to be under the protection of your brother Henrich and your uncles, who have made their way to Sir John, and will arrive in but a day or two to gather the others." I am relieved that our people gather together, for in times such as these, kin are to be much relied upon—for surely no one else is.

"Please accept my gratitude, Master Alguire, for your messages. I pray you will find safe passage when we are gathered by our people?"

"We shall not wait, for we leave upon this night. Because my father, brothers, and others sympathetic to our plight have been delivering messages to our friends, we fear this will soon be noticed. Already we have reports that punishment comes swiftly to those who give word."

"Well, then, please find a safe journey . . . and should you see my dear husband, tell him we are prepared and shall be ready for our journey as well."

Closing the door, I hear Hezekiah crack his whip upon the horse yelling, "Heeyah!" Galloping away as fast as his steed can carry him, the familiar sound of hooves upon the ground reminds me of the daily sounds that once were around us, yet unnoticed, and now among the most missed in this new world.

Just as I turn to begin my preparation for our own flight, a scream comes from the woods behind the house, "HELP US!"

Running to see the source, I make out a figure of a girl emerging from the thicket along the treeline, as she continues to scream. As she moves closer, the sun catches her face, and I see that her features are marred by distress and dirt, for, in her dishevelled state, she has evidently fallen on her way to us. I am still able to distinguish it is

Sarah Ball, young wife of Nathaniel Ball, whom I had seen in my own home but the day before when he gave us warning. With Hezekiah's words in mind, "reports that punishment comes swiftly to those who give word," I understand what it is that brings her.

Running to meet her, the children pouring out of the house behind me, wondering what all the excitement is, I reach her mid-field. She instantly collapses into my arms, sobbing, "He is hurt. He is hurt! They took him in the night, and he is hurt . . . and . . ."

I cannot understand what she is saying, for she is crying most inconsolably. Suddenly, she slumps down, holding her large, rounded belly. She is in her confinement and has not been seen in a number of months as she awaits the arrival of her first baby. I calmly tell her to show me Nathaniel.

The children dutifully follow me through the trail in the woods connecting our farms. Wanting to shield them from the sight we will find within the confines of the house, which is now coming into view, I point to the animals out in the field and tell the children to go see them while I "talk" with Mrs. Ball in the house. With the exuberance of youth and innocence Jacob bounds off. Mathias and Ruby, pensive and brooding, look at me, but as I nod, they follow to keep watch of him. In a time so unfamiliar, this moment strikes me particularly, and I feel a comfort in knowing Jacob is sheltered, thus far, and that there may yet be hope that Mathias and Ruby will not bear the full burden of understanding, for they, too, are young.

Entering the home, I look to a darkened figure in the corner sitting not upon a chair, but a milking stool, but cannot discern his face, as it is downcast. The body is covered in something unfamiliar . . . not clothing . . . What is it? Moving closer, I come to understand more fully about the cruelty of men's hearts when set upon a path such as ours. But sixteen years old and only newly married, Sarah is reduced to a child, looking to me for direction.

"Go and get some turpentine and lard, Sarah." She sets about doing as asked, which gives me time to cautiously approach young Nathaniel.

"Nathaniel, may I examine your wounds?" He looks up, and though the corner of the room in which he is sitting is dark, I see tears streaming down his face. He makes no sound. His eyes are childlike, pleading for help; he is wounded, to be sure, but it is not the wounds of his body that will not heal. His bodily wounds are horrific. Though his arms are spared, his entire body from neck to waist is covered in drying pine tar, obviously applied hot, by the blistering that rises upon his red, raw, burned body. He has not yet attempted to take off any of the white feathers which are fixed upon this. He was sat upon the stool by a desperate wife and left in his utter defeat.

Resuming her crying, she says, "This is all the turpentine I could find — it is not enough!"

I quickly reassure her, "It will be fine. We will work slowly with the lard; it will be less painful." I can see she is not looking at him, nor he at her. They seem as though strangers to one another. I realize if we are to set about our work, I will have to help both confront their fears. I grab Sarah's hand and in turn, Nathaniel's. "We must work as one, but to do so, we must look upon what has been done, and then set about to do as we must." I put their hands, one in the other, and I suspect what is for the first time since his arrival home in this state, look upon one another. Allowing his emotions to take over, young Nathaniel, but a year older than his wife, lays his head upon her body and the life that is within. Setting her hand upon his head reduces him to a child in the hands of his wife, and in this moment I realized that they are both very much still children.

"I knew them all," he says in a low, quivering voice. "The order came from my own father: Anyone caught sending out the warning should be — " He does not finish. With the agony of both body and soul-crushing humiliation at the hands of once-trusted companions, young Nathaniel has paid the price for his loyalty, not just to the Crown, but to his friends — to us.

Slowly, Sarah and I pull the feathers from the sticky substance. With each tug, Nathaniel winces in pain. The blisters seem to cover his entire body, making it unlikely the poor soul will be spared any further agony. It appears the necessity for using hot tar is to inflict just such pain, for it is not common practice to cause grievous injury, but rather humiliation. Looking at him, I am unsure which is worse, for they both are likely to cause lasting scars.

With the feathers removed from his body, we open the turpentine to clean the pine tar. My head begins to swirl about with the strong smell, making me feel as though I may fall off my chair. Sarah has an even more violent reaction and begins to retch. "We cannot use this." Quickly replacing the stopper in the bottle, Nathaniel has come to Sarah's aid. Guiding Nathaniel back to his stool, I show Sarah how to remove the tar with the lard. "We will need water to soak a cloth to soothe the burns." Sarah seems relieved to leave the room to fetch the water from the well. Sensing this may be my only opportunity, I warily inquire, "How is it you were taken and such a thing done to you; I believed you had left to meet your uncle and Sir John after your warning?" Looking forlorn at his sobbing wife outside the window, preparing the salve for his wounds, he does not look away from Sarah, but simply replies, "I could not abandon her."

I believe they will be fine, in time.

I leave Sarah to her work and gather the children from the field where they are playing. Realizing the day is almost done, and my time for preparation is drawing to a close, a renewed sense of urgency overwhelms me. "Come, now. We must get home before the sun sets." The path is darkening as the sky begins to welcome night. Dusk was at one time, not so long ago, a favourite time, when the sky turned many colours, and the stars would make their first appearances. Our little ones would tuck into their cozy beds to slumber, and I, with my beloved, would talk together of lovely things: the planting, the expected harvest, news of our friends and neighbours, and our children. Even in my memories of these times, I think of Nathaniel. *'Tis a dreadfully high price paid for his aid of friends and neighbours.* I could see that his pain was not so much the result of his grievous injuries, but the knowledge that it had been his father's order to bring justice to any who aid the enemy. I wonder if he had realized that "enemy" would take the form of his young son, not eighteen years of age.

As we near the fields where Peter should be; where he would now be feeding our animals, with Mathias often in tow . . . the little ones gather to my side at the apocalyptic sight before them, one holding the other. I look down the line at what has survived of our life . . . One. Two. Three. Sweetness and innocence in dark days.

CHAPTER 15

The early morning light appearing through my window is a grey blanket, just as a day of many days gone by. Knowing it is the quiet time when I will find him walking the land, I rise and go down to greet him.

Opening the door, looking out through the thick fog, I see him — as always — standing in his field, looking over all that he loves and is a part of. As the sun crests above the horizon, the greyness of the veil turns a brilliant white, and I run to him, only to have him fade away with the light. Standing at the fence, reaching out to touch what is not there, I slump to the ground and allow myself to give in to the despair — if but for a moment. I do not feel strong enough, brave enough . . . this is more than I can bear . . . and then a movement reminds me I must.

In my exhausted state, I have only imagined what was — what will never be again in this place. Now, just as I had my beloved leave me so suddenly in the night, I must prepare to leave our home; our place in this world. Pulling myself up, I shall no longer look upon this field, for I must remember it as it once was — not empty, as it is now; in this way, it will always remain lovely in my mind.

I turn to walk back to the house, alone but for my constant companion. Strangely, this provides a sense of comfort — a sense of shared knowing — somehow making it less lonely. The light and fog holds in its grip my tree, pink blooms now fully formed with just a few petals floating to the ground; it is these that catch my attention. The time of greatest beauty for my tree is coming to an end; the time for its work soon begins, and I know I will not see the fruit it will bear. I pick a flower from its branches and study the delicate nature of its form before I wrap it in my kerchief. I shall keep it close to me on our journey. I understand that my tree might not survive what is to come and I reach out to touch its trunk. I am conscious that it has no thoughts or feelings, but so many of my memories here are made sweeter by the presence of it. In darkening times, it provided a constant reminder that life goes on; it bloomed, bore fruit, went dormant and lifeless — and yet, regardless of the harshness of the winter, it bloomed again. For we must certainly be in the winter of our existence, and yet here is my tree in full bloom, glorious and beautiful. Perhaps we, too, will bloom again . . .

CHAPTER 16

May 20, 1780

Tending the glowing embers in the fire throughout the night, to provide only the most basic heat, I know the house will be cold and abandoned by morning. Even though the precise time of reckoning has not been foretold in Peter's missive, I feel sure it is upon this night that they will come. Yearning in vain that I should see the face of my beloved upon our rescue, I understand this to be too much to hope for. Hope is a delicate state that I had very nearly lost this morn, reaching for what is lost to me, but a small reminder pulled me back from an abyss I should have liked to sink into.

Though I endeavoured to stay awake through the night to ever be at the ready, I find myself startled at the sounds that now come from a distance. Unfamiliar, and yet too faint to hear in their entirety, I do not need further clarity to understand the time is nigh. I rush up the darkened stairs to gather my children and prepare them for the nightmare we are about to enter . . . for now I can hear the gates of hell opening, and as the sounds become louder, the familiarity of them strikes me to the core.

"Wake up, Mathias." I dread the reason I wake him so. He cannot imagine what he is about to endure, and yet I must ask him to relinquish his childhood as he has known it and help me to prepare Ruby and Jacob. He stirs and looks upon me with his blue-grey eyes so much his father's that I am injured by the loneliness they instill. As a sweet smile grows upon his face, I realize this may be the last time I see such innocence—beautiful in its unknowing—in my boy. "Come, we must away. Help me to prepare the children. Quickly now, Mathias. Tonight we meet friends who will lead us once again to your father."

Ruby and Jacob have begun to stir, as the noise outside our walls grows ever more menacing. As Mathias sets about clothing Ruby in layers of her warmest wear, which I had set out before bedtime, she does not resist, for it seems she is still half asleep. Her drowsy eyes show a glimpse of the brilliant blue that shine and sparkle with a beauty that makes one's heart ache at the sight. Golden ringlets about her face conjure angelic images, in such contrast to what I hear outside our home. At three, she is the meekest of my children, remaining quiet and shy since she first entered this world. She will do just as I ask, and yet for her I fear the most, as she is the most fragile — *was* the most fragile, I am reminded from time to time as I scurry about the room gathering more clothing to layer upon the children. It seems colder than on previous nights, and I fear they will be chilled upon the journey.

Jacob, not yet two years, babbles a little with the excitement of this night. He is wide-eyed, his blond hair tousled, and he is ready to dart from my arms as I dress him. A hearty and exuberant boy, these qualities, and his young age, will spare him the realization of what is happening; I pray that all may be forgotten, and that he will remember only what is to be in our new home. It is at once this exuberance that will aid in his survival, and yet, I fear will cause us grief upon the journey, should we have to shelter from the evils that lie in wait for us. What evils, I cannot fathom, but the dreadful sounds now filling the air confirm that my fear is well founded.

We quickly make our way down the stairs to prepare for our fate. Even as our time nears, waiting to learn who will come to our door is agonizing. I set Jacob upon Mathias's lap on the floor in front of the dying fire. Mathias holds tight, knowing Jacob would rather walk about, and already I see a change in him. He holds Jacob with one arm and puts his other arm around Ruby, who holds "Dolly" tightly to her as she listens intently to the sounds. As I check the knot of the bundle I have prepared of blankets for shelter, foodstuffs, and a few items of clothing, the urge to gather the children in my arms to comfort them becomes overwhelming, yet I must resist and be at the ready.

The rap on the door makes me jump. Ruby begins to whimper, but I do not move to comfort her, for our time here has come to an end and we are most instantaneously being set adrift in life. I open the door and am met by a most fearsome sight: a tall man covered in blood towers over me. He pushes his way in, closing the door quickly behind him. "I am to gather you and the children to be set upon the trail where you will be met by a guide. We must away at once." He does not wear a uniform, but his message rings true to Peter's words in his letter of but a day ago.

"Mathias, come now," I urge, as he stands in shocked disbelief of what he is seeing, unable to move. As the man gathers the little ones, roughly picking up Ruby and pulling Mathias by the hand so that he might follow, I pick up Jacob, who has run and hidden behind my skirt. Grabbing the bundle I have prepared, I am ready to leave.

"You cannot take that with you, for we travel fast."

"Yet I must—for we will have no means of survival should I not be permitted to take it along."

"Mrs. Eamer, you and your children will not survive if you do." At the sound of my name, the true gravity of the situation is made real. I have to trust that this man, a stranger to us, is our friend sent by Sir John—sent by my beloved to aid in our escape to freedom from this ill-fated place. With no time for one last look at our home, we pass under my tree and away into the dark of night.

In a state of alertness I have never experienced, I am suddenly aware of the many sounds, sights, and smells that at one time would have been unknown to me and confusing but are now revealed in clear, horrifying detail.

We stumble upon the frost-covered ground, blinded by the darkness, as no light is cast by the sliver of moon that hangs above us, yet our guide does not hesitate in his step or speed. I hold on to Mathias's hand, now, and he to Ruby's, as she has been set down, and we move as one to ensure we do not fall behind—instinctively knowing there would be no hope for us if this were to happen.

At our backs, the screams and cries for mercy carry clearly upon the winds. A mix of human and animal suffering, both equally wretched, both equally doomed, grow as the evil sweeps over the town, engulfing it in flames and death. The war cries echo, seeming to surround us. It is known that Sir John has had the aid of his Iroquois allies at his side, yet it still alarms me. Familiar, but equally menacing, voices yell words of retribution, and I know these to be Sir John's men laying siege to our once peaceful town.

Ascending the hilltop, which, once crested, will dampen the sickening sounds and spare us the sight of the destruction, I turn back and look down upon the valley where once we lived. Glowing upon the horizon, the barns and homesteads burn, casting light upon the souls of men and animals running in all directions . . . a scene of chaos signalling the end of this world. Smelling not the fresh air of spring, but the choking smoke of ruin, I step away from what was and look away into the dark ahead of us.

"Here, you must follow the path until you are met by your guide." This unknown man is lacking any emotion and barks his order as though we are but soldiers who will understand how to do as he asks. Standing in the obscurity of the forest we have entered, I cannot see his face and only know to follow in listening for his footsteps upon our path.

"And should it not be our guide we meet, what then?"

"'Then,' my dear Mrs. Eamer, is not something you will need to worry about."

In an instant, I feel him move past me, walking back along the path whence we came. As he crests the hill, I see his figure straight and tall. He ominously looks back at us for the briefest moment, the glow of the distant inferno casting a soft light upon his face. I can see the pity—and doubt—in his eyes. Then, turning, he steps off and is gone.

CHAPTER 17

Adrift upon the trail, the children are crying as the man leaves our company, for they seem to understand the precarious nature of our circumstances. There is little time for comfort; we must make haste. I stop, gathering them close to me to tighten their clothes about their necks and tying their scarves around their heads to stay warm on this cold night.

"There, my little ones, now we must set about on a great adventure," I whisper, "for we go to find your father this night." Unable to see their little faces, I can yet sense a change in their fear.

"Papa?"

"Yes, my little Ruby, Papa. Come now, we must away to our new home."

Struggling to find the trail, where once the silence of the darkened forest would generally set fear in me, I am now glad of it, as we move ever farther from the mayhem and bloodshed taking place at home . . . what was our home. I do not know where to go, but simply understand that we will be found; by whom, I do not dare to think on.

Without warning, I am suddenly aware of a presence standing in my path. The hint of a silhouette is evident only because my eyes have since adjusted to the dark. The silhouette is still, and I do not hesitate to approach it, for I know we will have no escape should it not be a friend. When we reach this person, who is not much taller than I, he turns, and we follow. The children do not react, for I am unsure they realize we now follow someone through the forest. The only sounds we hear are our own feet upon the path, and the occasional owl screeching in the night. The man leading us makes no sound, as though he is but a vision and not real at all. It does not matter; I follow regardless.

In what feels like hours, we finally come upon a clearing. As we leave the forest behind, I see the man and am not surprised to see that he wears the clothing of Sir William's and Sir John's acquaintances, the Iroquois. I have heard tell of stories of their ability to sneak up on unsuspecting people who would never know the cause of their demise. It would be but a flash, no sound to give warning. But this is not to be our fate. I sense we are being led to safety, as instructed, though he pays no attention to us, not even acknowledging our existence.

Our journey through this field, while welcome in the dim light it provides, brings the cold of night to bear on us in its entirety. Even in the advent of spring, the nights still hold the memory of a cold winter past. I cradle Jacob closer and feel his steady breath on my cheek; he sleeps despite the turmoil. Mathias, taking his duty as man of the family very seriously, wraps his arm around Ruby as she shivers.

Walking a good pace ahead of us, I marvel at our guide's unfamiliar look. I have never been this close to an Indian, my only exposure to his people from a faded memory of them passing our home in my childhood, and through the stories my father used to tell of his time when Sir William held great conferences upon his estate. My father would come home and tell us of all he had seen, and of their differing dress and customs. But, on this night, those stories are made real, and I find myself intrigued by this tale come to life. With long, black hair flowing freely, he does not resemble the men of our community. His long, fringed hunting shirt and manner of trouser are as I have seen our men wear, though his are made of buckskin, and not the linen I had oft sewn. He wears boots of the same, and from his stride it seems these are made for walking these very trails. He does not stumble about, as we do, instead seeming to know every step he is taking. While not tall for a man, he has an air of surety in his step that in unspoken ways reflects his certainty of where he is going; where he is taking us. He does not fear the night, for he walks as though it is his place; his home. My father's stories told of these people living amongst the trees and animals, which seemed unbelievable to us as children, for we feared what was in the forest; we feared a man such as the one now guiding us, for we also heard of their fierce nature. In the early years, my father told of times when friendship with the Iroquois was not always to be had, and the judgment they laid upon the settlers was most vicious. From his waist, I can see a barbaric and fearsome weapon dangling, but do not recognize it. Yet, just as he does not fear the dark as we walk, I do not fear him as I believe I should. I do not sense a fearsome nature, but rather a determination to bring us to safety, and so I must leave any doubt — and my father's stories — aside and follow.

Once through a small thicket at the edge of the opening, we are able to see the dim glow of a fire, and when we enter this small, enclosed clearing, faces look upon us that are as familiar as any I have seen in my life. That they are vacant with distress and exhaustion make them even more so, for they see the same in me as their eyes meet mine.

Of the small group of nine, only four are adults, the rest being children, who sleep under the careful watch of their parents. Our guide, who does not make any gesture to us, simply proceeds to a darkened area set back from the group, lies down, and sleeps most immediately. I see a place close to a woman who lies beside a sleeping child; her small, faint smile seems to welcome us destitute travellers.

But before I can make my way to her, a man approaches, introducing himself in a gruff voice: "I presume you are Mrs. Eamer, whom we have been waiting for?"

I nod.

"Well, I am Mr. VanAllen, and I will be leading you and the others to Quebec. Here are two blankets and some rations for your travel. We restock along the way when we can."

He hands me two woollen blankets and a haversack with the essentials for our trip. "Sleep now, for you are the last to come; we begin our journey in but an hour." He returns to his spot, propping himself against a fallen log that acts as his post, and he watches the fire intently.

Settling on one of the small blankets provided for us, I cover the children with the other, and they soon fall asleep, not from ease of mind, but rather from exhaustion. I cannot rest, hearing yet the sounds from my beloved Johnstown in my mind: the screams, the cries of grown men calling for their mothers, children calling out, and then the instant silence of those same voices. Though upon the trail I had imagined the faces of those bringing mayhem as those of the men who had burned our barns, helped by unknown dark forces, in the silence that now surrounds me, my mind begins to clear.

Not wanting to fall asleep, I open the haversack to take account of our food stocks. To my alarm, I realize the tin canteen of water, small parcel of salted meat, and bannock will not sustain us for long, and I wonder how to make these inadequate rations last. The final item lay at the bottom of the bag, and had it not been for the weight it held, I may have missed it in the depths. As I run my hand along its length, I grasp the reality of our situation, and not wanting to lay my eyes upon the weapon, leave it in its leather sheath in the confines of the haversack if needed . . . when needed. Startled by the movement around me, I realize that as I have been lost in thought, the dew has settled upon the children, and they begin to shiver in their sleep, which wakes them one by one, setting them to crying with the cold and miserable conditions. I pull them closer to me to provide what shelter I may in the open wilderness, knowing the comfort they need is none that I can give.

CHAPTER 18

With only a few restless, precious minutes of sleep, our guides quickly set about gathering their belongings and tell us to eat a little, as we will not be stopping for many hours. In the early light of day, I now see more clearly those we travel with. They set about a routine that is more familiar to them than I, and in not recognizing them to be those of Johnstown, surmise they are more seasoned in the journey, coming from other places in the valley. I set the children to rights and hand each a small ration of bannock and water, knowing that they will be hungrier than this; but not wanting to endanger our endurance in the days ahead, I sacrifice my natural sensibilities and do as I must. A sympathetic nod from the woman closest to me tells me I have done right. Her only child, a daughter, being about the same age as Jacob, also seems to understand this foreign practice and quickly sets about eating her small morsels. I dread the thought that my children will soon find this way familiar. When we were on the farm . . . but I shall not think of how it was before . . . we are now in a new world and I cannot pine for what cannot be.

"We stop for no one. We make haste to our destination, for we are at the mercy of rebels and savages until we reach Quebec." From the tone of his voice, I understand the warning he gives us, and as Mr. VanAllen glances in my direction when speaking these ominous words, I appreciate that while we may have guides, it is my resolve alone that determines whether or not we reach Quebec.

Rolling the blankets, I tie them with the twine in my haversack; I ready the children. The sun has not yet crested the horizon, but our guides are on the move. I take note that Mr. VanAllen does not consult with the Mohawk, for now I understand him to be so, as he refers to him simply as "the Mohawk," to those in our party. While both are leading us to Quebec, it seems it is done so very independently of each other, and of us; for, as yet, we have not heard our Mohawk guide speak. They are not friends, of this I am sure.

Already walking toward the forest, I secure the haversack and pick up Jacob so that we might not fall behind. Mathias and Ruby hold fast to one another and walk behind me as instructed. Throughout the night, I had pondered the placement of the children upon our journey. I could not determine if they remained safer in front of me — to face dangers before I can secure their safety — or behind, where we might not know the danger that lurks and shadows us. I eventually settled upon behind me, but for no other reason than I pray that if judgment falls upon us, they will not see the vile face that brought it to bear.

As we enter the thick forest, the trail seems to disappear beneath us, and we walk through thick vines, which catch us about the ankles, making many stumble and trip along the way. Always picking ourselves up quickly so we are not abandoned upon the trail, I soon find the burden of carrying Jacob difficult in keeping my balance. "Pick up a stick, for it will help you maintain the pace." The soft voice behind me is no more than a whisper, but this woman who had acknowledged me upon waking is now close at hand to deliver her message. I simply nod my understanding that talking will put us at risk of the dangers that live in this place. As my children are still in a state of disbelief, they have not made a sound, nor do I worry about this, as they, much as I, are simply existing — walking, doing as we are told — not yet able to fully comprehend what is happening.

Our journey continues for many hours, and, having found a sturdy stick as instructed by my unknown companion, I am able to make haste along the rough ground, for there is no trail upon our long walk. By and by, Jacob falls asleep, easing the strain upon me, creating small comfort in knowing I will not have to ease his every movement to avert his making any noise; for while the others can be reasoned with, the little ones in our group I fear for most and find myself fearing their natural ways. When we finally stop to rest at the edge of a field, I can see the dark, hazy silhouettes of mountains in the distance. Their majestic presence set against the softly rolling hills of places more familiar to us suddenly strikes me with the realization that if I am to endure, I will need to ask for God's help; for I find myself tired and weak after but a few hours. I pull out the bannock once more, leaving the meat to fill hungry bellies before bed, hoping this would ensure a more restful sleep.

As I sit quietly pondering the task at hand in but a few days, my attention is caught by a small tug on my arm. "You must eat something. We will not stop until dark."

"Oh, no; I am not hungry," I answer, hoping my untruth will not be discovered.

"If you will not eat, then drink; you will not serve your children well if you cannot keep up." As her own child lay upon her lap, my companion strokes her hair until the little one falls into sleep. She is looking over the view, perhaps wondering as I do if we will endure. Taking her advice, I take a sip of the water, which tastes strongly of tin but feels cooling in my parched throat. I want to keep drinking, but I stop after one sip, not knowing when we will come upon a resupply.

"Enough rest. We must make the foothills by nightfall." Mr. VanAllen sounds urgent, making me feel even more unsafe in our surroundings: there seems to be an unspoken warning. I notice the Mohawk has moved to a rise above us and looks most intently upon the horizon. In his scanning, I understand he knows of unseen dangers, and I heed the order and have the children take one final sip of water before we begin our trek anew.

The sun shines upon us and warms the day, though I shiver with what I presume to be the effects of our damp night outside, which has pierced my inadequate clothing, for I will not relinquish the one comfort of my children in the blankets provided to us. Now, even as the chill leaves me, I yet tremble. A sense of unwell consumes me, and I struggle to keep pace. The effort in carrying Jacob as he shifts about leaves me feeling unbalanced and furthers my grief. My body is heavy and cumbersome, and for a brief moment, I am reminded of why and cannot help but feel some delight in it.

We have finally stopped walking, and as Mr. VanAllen sets to building our fire, we are left to fend for ourselves in creating makeshift bedding in the last remaining light of day.

Pulling on the string, releasing the blanket from the haversack, I billow it with one great motion and allow it to fall flat upon the ground. The musty smell of its numerous uses overcomes me, and I hurry to retch as far away from our resting place as I am able to go. Jacob is crying, startled by my abrupt movement, but as I clean myself with the broad leaves of plants within the grasses, my young man has come to his brother's aid, and comforts him with songs he has heard many times as I rocked my babes—he being one not so long ago. This allows me to gather myself and take a short glance to the horizon, enjoying the beauty created by the fading light—the familiar mix of pinks and mauves that signal another day is done, and night comes. Looking at the same sky that rests above our home; the same sunset we have seen so many days upon our farm, I briefly recapture those moments and drift away in my memories.

"Mama?" Ruby has come to my side to ensure my well-being; looking at her, I know the miracle of our survival upon this day. Looking at the beauty of the sky, I give thanks with a silent, simple prayer for what cannot be expressed in mere words: "Thank you, dear God, for one more day."

With the little ones enjoying the salted meat I had spared until our night's meal, the fire, while not large, provides light and comfort in its warmth, just as the chill of night sets upon us like a blanket. The routine of an evening meal, even performed in this wild, unknown place, provides a sense of the familiar, and I find comfort in it—although my hunger reminds me that we sorely lack an abundance of real nourishment.

Ruby, who has been silent throughout the exhaustive walk, begins to whimper. I move to her and pull her onto my lap, wrapping my free arm tightly around her, as I hold my now sleeping baby in the other. "What is it, my dear, that troubles you?"

"Mama?"

"Yes?" Through her sobs I scarcely make out what she is saying, and must ask her to repeat.

"Is Dolly okay at home?" The reminder of home, created by our meal, has made Ruby miss what was, and the reality of our plight, and

Dolly's, sets in. Looking at my children, eyes full of desperation for reassurance, I realize my brave little ones yearn for home as I do.

"Dolly is fine. She is watching over everything for us now." The thought of her dolly thrown on the floor, abandoned and lonely — our home itself in the same state — makes me shudder, and I push the image from my mind, unable to bear it any further.

Suddenly, from behind us in the dark, our Mohawk guide returns with a bounty of fresh rabbits, a sight that creates some excitement among our group. Hunger seems to be a familiar condition to us all. I notice that Mathias is less affected by the prospect of fresh meat, and focuses his gaze intently upon the Mohawk. As he shifts back nearer still to me, I recognize fear and mistrust in his expression. Close by, now, I lean in and whisper, "He is a Mohawk of the Iroquois Nation, Mathias. He is one of our guides because his people live in these wild places. This is his home." Hoping this would ease his fears, I am glad to see that his concern has turned to surprise that I should know such things.

Quickly, however, his mistrust reappears. "Was it his people who were screaming the night we left?"

"There were many sounds of men that night, Mathias."

"But, Mama — " I stroke his back to encourage him to continue. "There were screams that didn't sound like . . . they scared me." With a tear rolling down his cheek, staring still at the Mohawk, I can see he is scared even now.

Knowing the sounds he is remembering, I explain, "They were war cries you heard. The Mohawks use the sound to gather their strength and set fear in the hearts of their enemies."

"But *I* was scared, Mama. Are *we* his enemy?" He is no longer troubled with the many sounds of his memory, but rather with the one unfamiliar man of strange costume and ways, skinning rabbits by the glow of the fire.

"No, he is not our enemy, nor were the scary sounds you heard the night we left the sounds of an enemy. What you could not hear, Mathias, in amongst those scary sounds, were the voices of Sir John and his men. They fought side-by-side with the Mohawks to make sure we could make our escape."

He suddenly looks at me with wide eyes full of realization. "But Papa is with Sir John. Was he there, too?"

Of this I do not want to think, for the sounds that haunt me are not of war cries, but the familiar voices of our people. "Perhaps, but he had a duty to help Sir John, and could not come for us himself." As his tears begin to dry up, Mathias will not take his gaze from our guide, but cautiously asks, "Is he Papa's friend?"

Remembering my father's stories, I answer, "Yes, and ours." He is not completely convinced, but I can feel Mathias relax against me and I know that understanding some truths of our situation might be helpful in easing young minds.

"Would you like to hear some of the stories my father used to tell of the Mohawks?" Two little heads nod, and I set Jacob, now heavy in my arm, down to sleep beside me bundled tightly in the warmth of the blanket.

Looking into the flames, which sputter with the juices from the cooking meat, I am brought back to a time when I was a child. A sense of safety fills me, and I am glad to find these feelings lingering still. "When our people first came to this land from the old country, we did not have much. The king—"

"Our king, Mama?"

"No, Mathias, a king in times past." I see he is disappointed. His eagerness to hear the tale is much as mine had been at his age. I realize I have not sat quietly with my children surrounding me in usual pursuits in many days, and this simple pleasure is a welcome diversion. "The king gave our people passage to his colony in America, and they were glad for it. We had to leave Germany, as our religious beliefs were not welcome. The king said he would let us worship as we wished if we would help to settle his lands, and so we did. We were given the chance to help Sir William work his lands, and if we worked hard, had the hope of one day owning our own land.

"And do we own it, Mama?"

"Yes, Mathias, we own it now." His pride is so evident and reminds me much of his father's as he had looked out over his land. "Papa must have worked well."

"He did, as all our people had.

"But the land we own now was not always Sir William's, Sir John's, or ours—it was occupied by the Mohawk and others. When the colonists first arrived in the valley, there was much conflict with the Iroquois, and Sir William, being a very wise man, knew this conflict would lead to disaster if it did not come to a peaceful end." I pause with the sudden realization that it was not the conflict with the Iroquois, but rather each other that had been our undoing. I look toward our guide and feel sorry that he, too, has had his once peaceful way of life disappear, and wonder if he has children who fear as mine do. I am surprised to find commonality with one so different, as I have never thought much about the life of his people. But with our lives depending on his guidance, I pray he understands better our desires to make it to the safety of Quebec.

As the plate of freshly cooked meat is passed for all to share, I take pause from my story to enjoy it. Rarely have I tasted such delicious fare, but I suspect hunger has created the delight in it. I wake Jacob to take of the extra food, knowing it will help greatly in warding off sickness upon our cold, exhausting journey.

As each finishes his or her portion, I tuck one little one beside the other to rest for the night. Ensuring they are well guarded from the cold with the blanket, I lean to kiss each little head that pitifully rests on hard ground.

"Mama, will you finish the story now?" It seems Ruby is equally taken with my father's tales.

In hushed tones, I continue. "The king trusted Sir William and put him in charge of all Indian affairs. This was a position of great importance, and Sir William came to see the Iroquois as his friends. From time to time, he would hold great conferences at Johnson Hall, and many of the Iroquois Nation would gather. The time of the gathering was always exciting. One time, when I was quite young, we had a group of Mohawks come through our back field on their way to one of the great conferences, and I, like you are now, was very afraid of these unfamiliar people. As they passed by our home, we watched from our windows, afraid to go outside while they were near. My brothers and sisters and I listened to the language they spoke—it was not our language that we spoke at home among our own people, nor the English that we speak now, but a language that my father said was as old as time itself. These people were 'ancients,' and their ways were very different from our own."

Sleepily, Mathias asks, "How?"

"Well, where we worship our one true God, they worship one they call the Creator. They believe much of what they receive comes from the earth, moon, sun, and even thunder." Invoking my father's voice in my mind, I see I hold the little ones in suspense, as he had us many nights by the fire of our home.

"Camps would be set about Sir William's lands, and a great fire, bigger than ours this night, would be lit on his front property, and all would gather around, the Iroquois sitting on blankets, and Sir William and his men seated upon benches at a great table that was set up for the drafting of the documents. Agreements of commerce and peace would be brokered during this time, which made our valley very successful compared to many. We lived in a land of plenty, only made so by the efforts of all who lived there."

Sensing the stillness about me, I look around and realize that my time spent in the memories of my father's stories has ushered all into sleep . . . except the Mohawk who tends the fire. Knowing he listened to my story, I wonder if he has heard the same tales in his childhood. It seems strange to find connection with this man from such different circumstances, but his quiet nature, and knowing of the places we have come from, provides a sense of shared history — much contrasted by the harsh and, at times, vulgar Mr. VanAllen, with whom I cannot compare my experience.

As the Mohawk is our sentry this night, I lie down and shut my eyes, just as a small movement rejoices in the nourishment we have, by the grace of God, received.

CHAPTER 19

As I slowly awake to the song of a red-winged blackbird welcoming another day, I startle, remembering I am no longer in the time "before," when waking was done in anticipation, not dread, as now. While I have faith, it is tested with every unfamiliar sound and assault on my senses: cold, hunger, illness, and even more so with every remembrance of home and the times that are to come. Looking down, I notice I cherish hope, even as I sleep.

Our journey continues as every day before. I do not yet know the name of my travel companion, who stays close to me, as I believe she takes special interest in my care. She is not my elder, yet I sense a wisdom forged of experience in this terrible new world. When we rest upon the third night of our journey, at the foothills of the mountains now towering in front of us, we finally make our introductions. "I am sorry we have not made acquaintance formally until now, but I wanted to give you time to settle into the regime of our journey. I am Elizabeth Hartle of Albany." She smiles sweetly, and her true and tender age shows through the facade created by necessity.

"I am Maria Catrina Eamer of Johnstown." It feels good to claim my home, even in conversation, and the familiar accent of our people allows us to find kinship among strangers. As our children sleep soundly about us, exhausted by the steady pace we have had to maintain, we converse in hushed voices throughout the night.

"This is my daughter, Isabel; she is but two years of age, but I am afraid she already knows too much for one so young. She does not smile or have the spirit she should . . . that she had . . ." My new friend trails off, and I see she is in places of "before."

I recognize it, for I am familiar with them — the places and times lost to us — though our hearts and minds would not let us forget; a seemingly unmerciful burden, for I am sure I might endure better if I could forget.

"My husband, Ezekiel, was taken almost a fortnight ago by the rebels. I will not call them friends, as they once were, for they most violently broke those bonds when they cast us out." Her voice is filled with rage, and I see the effort she exerts in trying to control this. While young, she is determined. In her is a strength of spirit I hope I will summon if I must. I am akin to her feelings, as the same lurk within me, and should I allow them to surface, I would be consumed by them. "We have never taken the side of the Crown, nor did we take the side of the rebels. We have lived and worked in Albany for generations, believing ourselves to be as all our friends and neighbours are — valued members of our community. When our alliances came into question, it was decided that we, as those of German descent, would more naturally take up the cause of the Crown because of old ties to when our forebears came to the colonies. It was in these sentiments, being expressed so freely, that Ezekiel realized we had never been part of the community as we had assumed. We were always outsiders.

"One by one, our friends and neighbours of German descent were sent to the Tory prisons for imagined and assumed sympathies. Then, as Ezekiel was closing down his shop for the day, for he is a blacksmith, he was snatched away. I was not able to see him beforehand and only heard of his imprisonment when they came to my door to inform me that we were no longer welcome and must leave at once. When I asked if I might bid him goodbye, they laughed at me and said, 'Not unless you are a good swimmer.' They had sent him to the fleet prison."

"What is that?" I asked, fearing the answer.

"A fleet of decrepit ships, gutted and made spare as to increase the suffering of the 'oppressor's minions,' they said, in such venomous ways that I should have liked to — " Elizabeth suddenly stops telling her story, looking instead at the little head of auburn curls. She pulls the sleeping one up to her breast and cradles Isabel with a gentleness that makes her anger dissipate most instantly. She looks back at me, tears welling in her eyes, and says, finally, "They took everything from us and cast us out as though we were refuse. And of my gentle Ezekiel, I know not his fate, but imagine death might be a more merciful end, should the stories of the fleet prisons be true . . ." She trails off, ending her story; such thoughts could only injure her further. "And your man: What has happened to him?"

"He is with Sir John," I say simply, not offering more. I am not sure which fate is worse, as I recall the sounds of Johnstown. I know she must have heard those same sounds in the air the night we first met, and we both understand what those sounds signalled. However, it was not of Peter I was thinking as she told her story.

I fear the answer to my next question, but find myself thinking about my parents in these times when I wish so for times past. "And of the prisons in Albany, are they as they say?"

She takes my hand for a brief moment, understanding why I ask, and simply answers, "They are."

In our silence of thought and remembrance, Elizabeth soon falls asleep with her head nestled close to that of her sleeping child. She seems to understand that sleep will not be the deciding factor of survival should menace appear, and so she slumbers soundly in the strange state of knowing nothing can be done; fate cannot be prevented.

Struggling to sleep, throughout the long night I find myself awake, as I have not been in days. I am more fully aware of our reality, and the haze of distress is lifting. While we had not wanted to participate in the rebellion that was now happening, it was forced upon us that we should choose. In our choice, we knew the consequences and somehow felt a little more in control of our futures. Then there were those who were simply cast out, as was my new friend.

Thoughts of my father swirl about, as the report of his imprisonment, combined with Elizabeth's stories, create a longing for the father of my childhood. I had always felt assured of his strength, and with all the dangers that must have been present, as they are now, I had not been made aware of these, instead spending my days in carefree pursuits. And of my mother, brothers, and sisters, I cannot know if they are on the same journey as I am, but on a different trail. I feel sure, if they survived the raids, they are experiencing much of what we now are. In this I take some comfort, for though we suffer now, there is some hope we may one day see each other again. Just as my little ones now lay their little heads upon me for comfort, I, stroking their hair in turn, yearn to be in the arms of my parents, back to a time of childhood and innocence. The world has come to show its truth, making me find ever more comfort in my memories, and in our Lord, who must be close to have brought us thus far. Of Peter, I cannot yet bring his image to mind, for it haunts me in most unsettling ways — its being linked to the screams I yet have lingering in my mind.

Whenever I shut my eyes to rest, they are filled with images accompanying the sounds that had come from my beloved Johnstown on the night we fled. No longer do I see the image of merely murderous rebels and their allies, but I see the faces of our neighbours and their children, meeting their fate at the hands of once-trusted friends, neighbours — and, even more horrific — family. The massacre that took place, from which we were spared, was not delivered by unknown forces, but rather known ones, making it even more unfathomable. They massacred their own people on the land they loved so much. I open my eyes to look upon my children, ensuring they are warm and resting, but equally for a reprieve from the truth unfolding in my mind. What was it like to look upon each other before killing? Was there a sickening realization of what one was about to do, or did it become impulse in the heat of battle? Did the will to survive take over? It is impossible to imagine the decisions of life and death being made by mere humans. Would God forgive this transgression on his powers? I am forever marked by the sounds of our animals suffering at the hands of our neighbours and friends; but the sounds I heard upon our flight were at the hands of Sir John and his men, at the hands of — I open my eyes and try not to think upon what has just entered my mind, for I cannot put this face, so clear to me now, in the midst of that ruin.

CHAPTER 20

My disposition is not so armoured in the need for strength and fortitude this day. I falter in focusing on why we journey, and am burdened by the misery of a steady, biting rain that has drenched us these three days. As though signalling the end of the hope spring generally brings, low, grey skies hang upon us and to the horizon as far as one can see before entering the forest once again. It has been a shock to feel the piercing cold at night, and though the sun appears from time to time, it cannot penetrate the chill we feel to our bones. The dimness of the forest makes the day seem as night, and though hints of green appear upon the trees, their leaves do not yet provide reprieve from this incessant rain.

Mr. VanAllen shows himself to be harsh. Even as we struggle with the slick mud that hinders our progress, he will not ease his pace and often threatens to leave us to the mercies of what may exist here in these untamed places. My skirt, heavy with wet and filth, makes the task of carrying my Jacob arduous. Small and unknowing, he often struggles to be let down to walk. I must keep him ever entertained, for he might begin to cry, should I not do so. With strict warning, Mr. VanAllen tells me the children bring the threat of a gruesome, untimely death, and that should I want to survive to see my husband again, I would do well to "control the lot." He has not spared Mathias and Ruby the details, and when we speak, they look at me with terror in their eyes. I, as their beloved Mama, should provide reassurance, but do not, instead allowing this man's words to set upon them as a way to spare them what he has warned. It is a most disturbing thought that my children should know of such things; that they should shiver with cold, whimper with hunger, and fall into a restless sleep not knowing if they would wake to dark forces setting upon them. Our miserable existence now, I pray, will be made a fair price for the life we will find in the king's lands.

Our days, spent in silent drudgery, see my new friend Elizabeth endeavour, as I do, to entertain her little one. One night, before we settle into our makeshift shelter, she shows me how the children might weave grasses along the way, which "keeps little hands and minds occupied in silent work." She seems so much more prepared for this journey than I. Any preparation of goods and supplies I had attempted would have been of ill use for what I could not have imagined was to be ahead of us. Abandoned, and yet resting upon the floor of our house—should our house still stand—the bundle is but a memory of my naïveté and inexperience.

I wonder if our neighbours have come into our house and been affected, as I am in its memory, by the emptiness of a once vibrant home. Or, has the tide turned, and do they look upon it as no more than the place where traitors to their cause had dwelt? I cannot reconcile myself to hate those I had once loved, even with the face of my father, lingering in a decrepit prison, fresh in my mind. These rebels have been possessed and do not fully appreciate what they have done, just as . . . just as Sir John and his men may not have known the injury they inflicted in the name of their cause.

My mind, full of noise and destruction, is interspersed with the faces of those loved and lost: those who wait; those of us here; those who might yet be. Stirred from my thoughts by a small movement within, I look toward those in my care, walking now but a few feet in front of me. The constant shifting of Jacob from one side to the other is necessary, unless he sleeps upon my shoulder, as now. I am forced to ignore the protests of another, and despite the discomfort, continue on. What necessities we were given are carried by Mathias upon his strong and sturdy back. He is an Eamer to be sure: tall and proud. I can see he already feels his purpose upon the journey. In his father's stead, my young man is surely a welcome companion and aid. Though drenched and dripping, the rain muffles our steps, and any noise we make affords a reprieve from our vigilance to remain silent. Just as I am about to return to the faces swirling about in my mind, Mathias turns and smiles, a reminder that even in his changed circumstance, he finds happiness in our being together.

At the end of another exhausting day of walking from dawn until dusk, we rest for the night in a grove of cedar. Their pungent scent leaves me feeling unwell, but their protection from the rain will allow for a respite from the constant barrage, which day after day wears us down. Only nine days from our home, I believe, and already it seems as though it were but a dream. I set about preparing the children's meal in the small shelter we have made of cedar boughs set against a fallen tree. The task seems familiar, yet the soggy bannock and tepid water are far from the life we had known. It surprises me that despite the disgust of the food; despite the hunger we all feel in every waking moment, we are glad for what little we have. An instinct I have not felt before is taking the place of my usual sensibilities, with a strength I did not know I possessed. These first days upon our journey, though miserable, allow me to more fully understand the task at hand, and understand what sacrifices may be necessary. There is a comfort in knowing what must be done; when choice no longer exists, there is peace. I now understand why Elizabeth seems calm: She had realized this early in her own journey.

With the rain finally easing, Mr. VanAllen sets about building our nightly fire. Small, and threatening to extinguish as wet branches hiss, the small flame takes and begins to billow white smoke. This seemingly customary practice signifies one more day is done, another day closer to Peter, and though many days yet lay ahead of us, each leads us to life once again.

CHAPTER 21

Having made our way to the mountains that signal our greatest trial yet, we now follow a well-trod Indian trail that improves our pace, for we do not stumble and fall as in the lowlands. However, it reminds us that we are not the only ones in these seemingly desolate places. It is hard not to contemplate who has cleared our way—friend or foe? In these times, they are often one and the same. In parts where we veer from the path to avoid unknown dangers, we are often forced to tread through thicket and mud, which is difficult and painfully slows our progress.

Our travel companions, a Mr. George Burnhart, his wife, and four children, three sons and a daughter who seem to be of the ages of four to nine years of age—do not associate with us. From their manner of dress and custom, we believe them to be of privileged society, who do not generally associate with people of our humble sort. Mr. VanAllen caters to Mr. Burnhart in a most curious way. He seems to forget we are all equally at the mercy of our circumstances and provides for this family's particular needs as though he were a doting servant. I have come to conclude that, unlike Elizabeth and I, who will have wages paid by the Crown upon our safe arrival, Mr. Burnhart is paying not only for passage but for a certain degree of comfort. The dour nature of the family, even children as young as these, regardless of our current state, seems to have been their way prior to our journey under the strict hand of Mr. Burnhart. Though we travel as one, we still hold fast to the familiar social accords that exist in civilized society—even in uncivilized surroundings.

On the days since we have entered the mountains, as we move ever higher, the weather seems to be lagging behind our late spring. No longer does the dew merely settle upon us as we sleep; it crusts in the frigid air, leaving us to huddle closely together by the fire. Elizabeth and I put our children between us and form a protective barricade around them, taking only what little blankets we need to ward off the sickness that can come of cold and damp. We have learned to use the boughs of the pines that surround us now as an added source of protection. Yet, despite the protection from the chill, the heavy, pungent odour of the freshly broken pine is overwhelming to me at times, and I find that I retch with every breath. I cannot understand why such a common smell creates such a violent reaction. A small mercy is in the exhaustion I feel at day's end, for it swiftly lulls me to sleep; yet not always a restful sleep, as my dreams are vivid and affecting. They leave me unsure of my state, as being awake or dreaming, upon the morning. I often find my ability to keep moving along the trail is through God's hand alone, for I am weary and unable to retain much of what little food and drink I take. Elizabeth watches over me closely; I recognize she is aware of more than I have shared, for her counsel to keep up my strength is tinged with a voice of knowing.

We have resupplied twice, finding small mountain lakes to refresh our bodies and canteens. Our Mohawk guide often disappears for many hours at a time, and we are unsure of his return, but nightly, we are glad to see him bring fresh meat for our sustenance. He has become an unexpected comforting presence, and though we have journeyed many days together, he has yet to speak to us. His confidence and calmness of spirit are in contrast to Mr. VanAllen's, who frequently becomes impatient with our little ones and shoots us looks of disdain. As they have become more familiar with their circumstances, I have witnessed a reawakening of the children's natural wonder.

By day, I carry Jacob so that we might keep our pace, for he remains unsteady on his feet on such terrain. Yet even as my strength falters, I somehow carry on as though it did not, for I am aware of the stares of others upon me; upon my oft-forgotten condition — for the reminder of it rarely makes its presence known. My own little ones pay no mind to the distress upon my face, for they are hearty and young, finding a measure of fascination in our new surroundings. By night, I close my eyes sporadically, as with increasing fatigue my anxiety has reawakened in a most distressing way. Always listening, watching, in the blackness . . . hearing twigs snap . . . perhaps the sound of approaching rebels hunting Loyalists . . . or families such as my own, struggling to make their way to the king's lands . . . wolves or coyotes . . . all or none, all are fearful.

It has been a fortnight since we last saw our home. When I do close my eyes, I dream of the time "before" and am soothed — if but for a moment. Burdened by a growing necessity to sleep, it is essential I fight this so that I might remain aware of our present circumstances, leaving little time for comforting thoughts of "home." What must be done to ensure the safe arrival of those entrusted to me; to arrive in Quebec, and the arms of our king, and to my Peter, is uncompromising. Though I hunger and thirst, I will not take more than is necessary. In the dark of the night, I reflect upon the voice of my new friend Elizabeth, "You must, dear friend, for you will sacrifice more than you may be able to bear." If I were to allow it to enter my mind — beyond what I must — I could not bear any of what has come to pass. But, we are upon this path, and we all do as we must. Our "journey" is but an existence that we must travel to once again attain life. Now, there is no joy, no sadness, no fear as it ought to be; we merely walk, endure — exist.

And now, I must sleep. All is still . . . "All" are still.

CHAPTER 22

We have crested many hills with seemingly no valleys, ever upward, ever colder and harsher the trails, but now our first sign of civilization comes into view in the valley below us. We began this day earlier than most, so as to make our way through rivalled territory at a breathless pace. Already an hour into our day's journey, the sky is just taking on the now familiar hues of pink and orange as the sun makes its gradual ascent into morning.

Seeing the wafting smoke rising above the treeline, much like a thread reaching skyward, we sense it is not the comforting smoke of a homestead fire, keeping a family warm inside, but the residue of what I expect will be another reminder of how precarious our current state of life is. I have seen these traces of what Mr. VanAllen callously referred to as, "another burned-out shell," as though he were keeping a macabre record of destruction, a cruel pastime he seems to take some pleasure in. We have so far mercifully been spared the detail by distance from what I can only imagine once existed in a peaceful setting. From our current course, it is evident we will not be spared the detail this time. Steadily, as though led by a guidepost—this one of smoke—we move ever closer. My impulse to protect the little ones from what we will encounter sets my mind racing as to how we may pass by without gazing upon what is now in place of where life had been.

Exiting the forest into a well-maintained pasture, the crunching of the white, frosted blades of grass underfoot in the hollows that dot the land seems unnaturally loud. Our guides have warned us to keep quiet as we proceed forward, knowing that the foe who has caused this may very well be near. It is our Mohawk guide who scans the horizon, occasionally stopping to set his hand upon the ground, looking at I know not what, but seeming satisfied that we may proceed. Each time he stops, scans, and bends down, I almost expect to hear war cries coming from the forest. Having heard them only once as we fled Johnstown, this memory and the stories of some of our travel companions who have survived such attacks give me reason to fear that every tree could disguise death lying in wait. These open fields we now walk through, where animals had once grazed, seem to expose us to perilous danger lurking in the inky darkness of the forest surrounding us on all sides.

While I have never felt a measure of safety on our journey, the little ones, and their care, have kept me focused on my duty as their protector. I accept that it may not be within my power to ensure their bodily safety, but their spirit—youthful and alive—is my duty to protect. Holding tightly to my hand, they feel comforted by my presence alone, and do not require me to whisper words of encouragement; already they know much of what is demanded of them. When we arrive in our new homeland, these little spirits will move forward in lightness of youth—not with the scars that I feel gathering upon my own spirit with every troubled, sleepless night . . . with every bend of this Mohawk to the ground to feel if fear courses through the earth itself.

At the edge of the pasture, we are once again swallowed by a short, but heavily forested, trail that soon opens up to reveal the shell of the homestead. Barns blackened and smouldering, as my own had been, rest but a few steps away from where a home once stood. These were the source of the smoke; the hay being the last to relinquish the evidence of what happened in this place. The home, unrecognizable as such in its current state, is but a heap of charred remains. No life exists here. From the steady pace of our march, the unchanging faces of those in our party, it is understood by all that there is nothing to be done . . . no one to search for . . . no one, and nothing, to be helped.

I am relieved that the children will not see any horror in this place, for it seems the family is taken, perhaps to prison; for surely this is the work of rebels . . . surely, they were only taken. The scene is familiar to them. They have seen our barn burned, heard our animals scream out, and witnessed the blackening of the life we are leaving behind. With all this familiarity—this offending familiarity—the image that now floods my mind is my apple tree standing untouched as I looked upon it for the last time. It gives me a glimmer of hope that it has survived — that something has survived — and while it feels frivolous to think such thoughts, it is all I have to cling to now.

Tripping over a rock sticking out of the ground jars me back from the memory of my tree. Looking up, I realize we are about to be consumed again by the dark forest. As my eyes adjust to the changing light — to the blackness — I suddenly see that the reality of what happened in this place is about to make itself known in a most grievous way.

The body lies unnaturally in the underbrush about twenty feet down the extremely narrow, rough trail. Instinctively, I understand it is a member of the family who had lived in the ruined home. From the size of the bare, porcelain legs that extend from under his muddy, blood-soaked nightshirt, it is obvious this is not a man, but a boy of about ten.

I must shelter my precious ones from this sight. Aware they do not yet see it, as their pace remains steady and they look in the direction of an eagle calling in the distance, I rapidly move to the inside of the trail, closest to the boy, and direct their attention to the sound they are seeking, which is thankfully away from the sight. Walking past the boy, my skirt brushes against his white legs, and I find it impossible to look away. It is hard to comprehend what I am gazing upon. Face down in the dirt of the thick, leafy undergrowth, this poor soul comes into full view revealing a confusing scene. The head, devoid of its scalp, looks unnatural. While it no longer bleeds, it is obvious from the amount of blood that has seeped into the nightshirt, leaving only the bottom part all that remains of its natural light colour, that this poor, unfortunate soul had stood at the time when this wound, ragged and raw, was inflicted. As the blood dried, it turned black, with but a few tufts of golden hair visible upon the left side. It is still not enough to make me scream out. In its current condition, I cannot see a boy in my mind's eye. This is simply a body. The only humanity still evident is the outstretched arm seeming to reach for an unattainable reprieve from its fate; a haunting reminder of the spirit that had struggled until the end for salvation — a salvation denied.

Within moments, we pass the body. Though there had been little talk throughout the early morning, the lack of it now seems particularly profound. Our guides do not pause or ease the pace of their stride, but walk as though nothing lay there beyond the trail. With the little ones shielded by my skirts and the pace of our walk, they were spared the sight of what I had but briefly brushed up against in my effort to ensure I was the only witness among my people.

A question lingers as we trudge along the trail once more: Had Peter been part of the group that had laid such destruction upon this family? Had he witnessed the atrocity? The laying to waste of homesteads and whole communities was the reason we held so strongly to our convictions and stayed neutral for so long. Our convictions, our God, would not allow it, but had it come to pass regardless; was this an inevitable fate running its true course? Like the body now lying silent upon the ground, undignified and once desperate, am I, too, walking the trail fate has set for me?

My head aches with all the memories of my life "before" and the thought of Peter, perhaps just out of reach somewhere in this very forest. Suddenly I am overtaken with sickness and lean to my side and retch. In my prior existence, the boy's body upon the trail itself should have triggered such a reaction, but now it is just the usual result of my condition. Am I becoming hard? In the beginning, I felt it was too much to bear, but quickly realized I must for the little faces yet looking skyward for their bird. My survival, I have become acutely aware, is intrinsically linked to theirs.

Where once I had dreaded the departure from our beloved home, I am now relieved that the fate of that family, which—I heard Mr. VanAllen inform Mr. Burnhart—"lies within the shell of their home," but for one, has not befallen the precious ones now under my care during our exodus.

It amuses me how the difference between the words "journey" and "exodus" conjure images of two vastly different circumstances. For with the little ones, I must use the word "journey," so that they might find adventure in place of the fear that "exodus" demands. It is a master without gentleness of spirit. It is fraught with fear—it damages and scars.

Oh! I grab a tree for support until the sharpness passes. It catches my breath and demands even more attention in these times than the need to move on. Yet, it must be brief so others will not take notice. I have come to notice the sidelong glances of those in our party upon my growing body. In their silence I am comfortable that we have an understanding. Putting my hand on the side of my secret, I pat gently and it subsides.

Looking skyward to the eagle they now spot darting through the canopy of the trees, Mathias and Ruby have settled into the rhythm of the march and are now ever so slightly ahead of me, exploring the plants growing along the trail. In such usual endeavours of childhood, I am pleased to see resilience. They often marvel at the smallest spring flower, such as the one Ruby runs to give me, or find excitement in the sound of scurrying animals along the trail, and birds gliding over-head. These sounds, which create such wonder in my children, do not entrance the adults in our group, for every sound, even the most commonplace, instills unease.

Oh! The sharp pain in protest overcomes my ability to continue. Elizabeth moves to speak with Mr. VanAllen. Suddenly he turns, announcing in a stern voice, "We rest for a few minutes." I instantly slump to the ground at the sound of our guide's allowing for this pause. Immediately attending to my side, Elizabeth sets my little ones and Isabel with her own canteen of water, telling them to sit quietly together. My head swirls, and I cannot seem to concentrate on what is happening. Taking water from my haversack, Elizabeth says in a hushed voice, "I have seen you over these past days give all your food to the children and take none for yourself. You must ensure you take your share, dear friend."

I forcefully protest in an equally quiet manner, "My little ones will not be deprived of these few morsels and the remaining water of our last resupply. It is ever my charge that I should ensure the children have every advantage to meet the brighter future that awaits them."

"Yes, my dear. You must ensure that 'all' your children have this opportunity." She does not address me directly, but fixes her gaze upon the one yet to be.

Having recovered enough to be back upon the trail, I wonder if we are all on the same path.

CHAPTER 23

The scene of but two days ago seems to have left its mark upon Mrs. Burnhart, as she increasingly voices her concern and looks wildly at the trees within the forest throughout our long days. Where once Mr. VanAllen was ever at this family's summon, he now is equally irritated with them as he has been with us and our children's occasional noises. Even our Mohawk guide now keeps a wary eye on the situation—for it is most evident that with every hour, this poor woman's state of mind deteriorates.

Rounding a bend in the trail, a deer leaps away in surprise at our presence. At this, Mrs. Burnhart screams and will not be comforted. Mr. VanAllen turns and quickly makes his way to Mr. Burnhart, who is trying to console his wife. It is strange to see this seemingly harsh man be so tender with her. In his actions, it is obvious he loves her deeply, and perhaps much of the air he put on during our travels thus far has been to set her mind at ease. "You must stop her," Mr. VanAllen seethes.

As Mrs. Burnhart cries uncontrollably, her husband continues in a soothing, but ever more desperate voice, "Annabel, please. Please take comfort, my dear. We are safe."

"That boy—that boy—the same age as our Thomas, had no scalp. He lay in the dirt with no Christian burial. We shall all die upon this trail as he did!" She is now hysterical, and in a flash Mr. VanAllen turns to her slapping her so violently it knocks her to the ground unconscious. Mr. Burnhart does not protest, as it is obvious to all there is no alternative.

With my children scurrying to my side startled by the sudden onset of such madness, I look toward their children and cannot discern any marked change in their expressions—none cry or make a motion to aid their mother. I immediately understand this family had seen more—experienced more—than I had presumed. While they are of noble stock, their mannerisms are now revealed not as an air of superiority but anguish; even now, the children are not stirred.

Mr. VanAllen turns back up the trail to meet the Mohawk, who has silently watched all unfold. For the first time that I have witnessed, they consult with one another, though I cannot hear what they say. I see the Mohawk looking up at the ridge above us, and Mr. VanAllen's eyes follow, giving us even more cause for concern. As the Mohawk slowly creeps up the hillside, Mr. VanAllen rushes to Mr. Burnhart, "We cannot stay here any longer. We have been hunted these several days by the Oneida, whose result we saw but two days ago. Your wife's madness calls attention to us that we can ill afford if we are to arrive in Quebec."

Elizabeth and I look desperately at one another, understanding the danger we are in, which seems closer at hand, now. We have been witness to its result, and even our imaginations of what lies ahead of us cannot create visions as dark as we have seen in reality. "But my wife lays unconscious, sir; she must rest." Mr. Burnhart's voice is pitiful and pleading, seeming to know there is little choice.

"You are welcome to stay here, Mr. Burnhart, as you wish. The rest of us leave now."

"I shall pay generously for our rest."

A wicked smile crosses Mr. VanAllen's face. "Much good it will do me when I am dead." He turns, walking the trail as before. Our Mohawk guide disappears into the forest, but we know he is not far and can yet see us, though we may not see him. We cannot aid this poor woman, for we have our own children to care for, and will be left without hesitation if we do not follow now.

Mr. Burnhart, a man not twenty years my elder, a man with a nature of business pursuits and seeming little experience in the ways of working the land day and night, puts the haversack he has been carrying on his youngest boy, as the others already carry sacks of provisions, and cradles his wife to carry her. It is obvious her unconscious state makes this task excessively trying, but through sheer will and desperation, he keeps pace.

Within an hour, Mrs. Burnhart begins to stir, and, mercifully having distanced ourselves from the most imminent danger, Mr. VanAllen allows us to rest. Mr. Burnhart, drained of his energy, slumps to the ground looking much older than his years, soaked through with the sweat of his exertion. Mrs. Burnhart, now consumed by fever, has her eyes open but does not speak. Her eyes are much changed. As wild as they had been, she is now distant in her mind and no longer comprehends this reality. I envy her, for she does not fear as before; she does not think as before; she is far away from these frightful places . . . she is in a place of silence; not peace, but silence.

Elizabeth hands Isabel to me and quickly makes her way to Mrs. Burnhart, pulling her off her exhausted husband, who cannot exert any further effort to do so himself. Bringing her own canteen to Mrs. Burnhart's fevered lips, she forces her to take sips of water. Mr. Burnhart is soon tended to by his daughter, who has slowly stepped from her state of shock to take her mother's place, though she is no more than six years of age.

Now close to dark, the Mohawk reappears on the trail in front of us, with rabbits in hand. He waits for us to follow to our resting place for the night.

We travel not an hour, with Mrs. Burnhart hoisted upon her husband's shoulder in a most undignified manner, all expectations of propriety having given way to survival. As we reach a small, rocky outcrop at the edge of the mountain, Mr. VanAllen, no longer catering to the Burnharts, builds the fire, while the Mohawk prepares the meat. Elizabeth and I place our children together and sit, as we always do, on the outer edges to create our barricade. Accustomed to our usual routine, each performs her tasks absentmindedly . . . we are transformed and have left who we were far behind; many steps upon the trail now separate us from that life.

Eating our welcome, but meagre, meal—for our bannock has run out and we now rely wholly on what comes to us from the Mohawk—we watch Mr. Burnhart tend to his wife, now drenched with the effects of the fever. She is delirious, but makes no sound, only staring at the stars above her, fixedly and with no attachment to this place or time. Her daughter dutifully supplies the meat and water to her brothers, all seeming to understand that sadness or fear of their mother's state will serve no purpose. As Mr. Burnhart waves away the water he is offered by his daughter, I notice she has the very look of her father, raven hair untamed, though her father's now has hints of silver. Her eyes, green as her mother's, though sallow, have life in them yet. It is faint, but I see her spirit lurking behind the curtain of fear, despair, and the terrible things she has seen; for she is sorry for her father's refusal. I have not taken much note of these children, for my own have been my only concern, but now, at this crossroads on our journey, I look upon them as if for the first time. The boys, fair like their mother, are older than their sister, but seem more lost. This little one stands out as a perfect combination of her parents; I hope her fate is not to be that of her mother.

Mathias keeps a wary eye on the scene, and though I do not look at him, I can see that he looks at me with concern. I continue with our usual routines, praying this will ease his mind. The children, even the Burnharts', who kept close watch over their parents, soon fall asleep with exhaustion. Our Mohawk guide takes his rest in the dark, set apart from our group, and Mr. VanAllen sleeps soundly by the fire, leaving Mr. Burnhart to hold his wife as Elizabeth and I look on.

The ridge affords a view that seems unending, and in the blackness, millions of stars dance about, making the sky seem alive. Sporadically, they flash by leaving a long white trail for just a moment; I delight in the unexpected surprise, a feeling I have not experienced in many days . . . weeks. I resolve to stay awake with this pitiful man tending to his dying wife. I am not alone in doing so. My friend Elizabeth seems equally captivated by the reverence of this night, and the beauty that now sets upon Annabel Burnhart. In our silent vigil, I study this woman at her most vulnerable, and am astonished at how the strain and harshness of her features change markedly as she is consumed by madness. As she gives way to the abyss of delirium, now making her soft and the colour of porcelain, she is ethereal. Her once wild blue eyes, full of fear and mistrust, no longer look to the heavens with a dull, lifeless gaze, but have slowly and finally closed. While she breathes, she is no longer of this world; she is but a ghost in this place. Her hair, always pulled tight and kept in perfect order until these last desperate days, is now flowing about her face and breast . . . her hair much the colour of my own, her eyes much as my own; the similarity sends a shudder through me. I had not pondered my own mortality until mortality is shown to be fleeting in these many days. Even then, it has not been until now that I suddenly realize I am as equally at the mercy of this life as Annabel.

A few hours into the vigil, it is over. Mr. Burnhart looks toward us with tears in his eyes, and I move to inform Mr. VanAllen. He wakes with a start, but rises quickly, going to aid Mr. Burnhart. He knew, as we all did, that Annabel Burnhart's journey was to end on this ridge, under a blanket of dancing stars.

With the two men disappearing into the black forest carrying the body, I look over at the Burnhart children, seeming no more than babes in their slumber, and regret that their journey in life has most irrevocably changed. Elizabeth and I look at each other with under-standing, and lay our heads upon the rock to sleep surrounding our precious ones.

CHAPTER 24

The rough earth on which we tread shows little evidence that others have taken this route before. I feel sure we are staying off the trail for a purpose, and I see the Mohawk and Mr. VanAllen keeping a wary eye on the forest surrounding us. It is an understanding that all, even the youngest among us, have: to survive, we must stay absolutely silent. I see that Mathias notices with great interest the proximity of the Mohawk guide, which is unusually close. He most often disappears into the heavy forest, scouting our way and, I suspect, looking for those who hunt us. But throughout this morn, he remains close and often looks behind us as though the forest itself might swallow us at any moment. Gloomy and damp, my Jacob buries his head in my neck to shield himself from the anxiety he senses, while Ruby holds my hand with a tight grip. They do not explore the forest and look for the creatures that live within, for this place seems ominous.

We feel as prey and must mask our existence with silence, much as do the animals that we surprise daily upon the trail, emerging most unexpectedly from the trees; we fear men would be able to do the same. This had most undoubtedly played upon poor Annabel Burnhart's mind these last days of her life. Such a burden to carry; such images we have seen, it almost seems a small mercy for her to have found an end to such suffering. Yet, one only has to look upon the sullen faces of her children to see they suffer in knowing her death was miserable and her burial un-Christian. Such memories—as a nightmare made reality in the world in which we exist—must surely mark them in most lasting ways.

Mr. Burnhart has been relieved of his haversack by the oldest boy, for he seems in no condition to carry anything. He is still exhausted from carrying his poor wife but the day before; and yet, I am certain he would do it again, should he have the opportunity to have her in his arms now. He is most distraught. And though he does not cry, his face is strained with desperate sadness and longing. As I observe his children, who walk silently in front of him, I cannot help but find them remarkable creatures; for when given the chance, when duty requires it, they seem to have the knowledge of adults. Even his young daughter does not request her father's comfort; she simply understands each must walk their own path with grief.

Suddenly, Mr. VanAllen and the Mohawk stop and look about wildly. It is not a noise that has alerted them, but rather the absolute silence of the forest. All life has seemed to disappear most instantaneously. It is disconcerting how the *absence* of sound can impart even more fear than the sound the unknown creatures of the forest make. I look at Elizabeth, but see she is as confused as I. The fear on the faces of each of our party is overwhelming; even Mr. Burnhart regains his senses. I gather the children to me and await whatever lurks in the shadows. As I pull Mathias close, I feel the long, hard object protrude from the haversack, and am thankful that it has made itself known to me. My mind is imagining the unimaginable, and all I can think is how I shall save my children. I quietly reach into the bag and pull the long knife from its sheath. Ruby looks at me in horror, and I give her a faint smile at her to reassure. I feel as though no one else exists in the overwhelming silence. The forest is closing in on us, and I have but a single thought: "I must save my children at all costs." As I stand waiting for judgment to descend upon us, the fear leaves me and in its place there is resolve as I have not before experienced. I feel alive and most aware of all that is happening—the anticipation provides strength in a peculiar way.

"Traitors!" The screams of the men who jump from the rocks ahead of us on the trail break the silence in such a shocking manner that, though there are only three of them, their sound is deafening in the utter silence. I thrust the children behind me and ready myself for the fight I will mount in defence of my precious ones. As though we are of one thought, Elizabeth and Mr. Burnhart take up positions at either side of me, each with knife in hand, and we create our protective barricade. Mr. VanAllen and the Mohawk rush to meet our attackers head-on.

"Die, you traitors!" yells the first man heading toward our group. "Liberty for America!" screams the next. But these two noisemakers are not the ones I fear most. The third man, not but a boy yet, has murder in his eyes, and in his silence shows a terrifying resolve. The first two men, seeming to believe their noise will set fear in our hearts, are quickly overwhelmed by the ferocity of defence by Mr. VanAllen, who has shot the first dead, and the second who has been clubbed about the head, by the fearsome weapon we saw the Mohawk carry upon our first night on the trail. It is most effective.

The children, terrified by what they are witnessing, hold tightly to my skirt. Shoving them away, knowing if I must fight, I cannot have them holding on to me, Jacob grabs my hand as I turn to push him back, and I struggle to free myself. The older Burnhart boys thankfully drag him from me, though I hear him fight them. His screams are but noise in my head, and I cannot focus on these. Safeguarding the younger ones, I hear one of the boys say in a stern and commanding voice, "Come now, huddle here. Our mothers and father need to fight." Feeling my absolute right of defence of these children in this moment, that is exactly what I intend to do.

The third attacker, with no regard for the loss of his companions, heads swiftly but silently in our direction as Mr. VanAllen and the Mohawk make sure the men they have subdued are in fact dead. We all raise our knives in unison. In reaching us, I can feel the warm breath and spit upon my face as he hisses, "Sir John has taken what I love most, and now I shall pay him back in kind and take his people from him!" With the raising of his gun, I tighten my grip upon the handle of the knife and raise it to meet his onslaught. A sudden flash of buckskin appears in front of our eyes, and with strange gracefulness in his execution, the Mohawk silently takes him down. Seeming unreal, I cannot look away as the knife disappears into flesh. Despite the intervention, his motion carries him forward and he falls upon me and Mr. Burnhart, his blood covering us as he slumps at our feet.

Standing close, but knowing his work is done, the Mohawk does not continue his attack. Sputtering blood from his mouth, hate lingers in the eyes of our attacker. Though he may have been a boy, tending fields, working along with his father at one time, hate had long ago killed that boy, and what now lay on the blood-soaked ground was the result.

I have never seen a man killed before, nor would I have expected the relief in its outcome, but I cannot feel pity for one who would have taken away what I love most dearly. Looking behind us at our children huddled with the older Burnhart boys, now releasing their grip on the youngest ones, we gather them and walk past the bodies, leaving them where they lie, and simply continue to walk on. With the final, hateful words of our attacker in my mind, flashes of Johnstown — the pillaging and murdering at the hands of Sir John and his men — clash in a realization that the victory of righteousness is paid for with the souls of men.

The demeanour of Mr. VanAllen and the Mohawk has changed, and as I see the familiar trail come back into view, I know the danger that had been hunting us was left in the thick of the forest to be consumed and forgotten.

CHAPTER 25

There seems to be a new collective determination among our group. When tested in such ways, it creates bonds among strangers, and though we are not friendly, save for Elizabeth and I, we know we shall defend our group as one. I dare not say Mr. VanAllen has improved his opinion of us, but I sense he has gained some respect for the lengths we will go to do our part in protecting our children. I suspect he feared, as I, too, would once have believed, that women in particular would be of little use in such situations. But the need to protect my children was overwhelming and filled me with such strength and courage that it seemed to come from God himself. I am sure that when necessary, it can be summoned, but it leaves me feeling the mystery of such things. I wonder if this will be enough to overcome the illness I am taken by. It is obvious to all that I am in a more precarious state than others.

In reaching a safe distance from our troubles, we stop to rest.

"Why did the man scream, 'Liberty for America,' Mama? Are we not free?" As young as he is, Mathias is trying to make sense of his current circumstance—and why men, so familiar in their appearance to what he has known, should treat us as an enemy. There is little sense can be made of it.

"Yes, Mathias, we are free, but many of our neighbours believe the king treats them unfairly, and they no longer wish to be under his rule."

"Well, then, whose rule shall they be under?" His innocence is evident; he cannot imagine such a thing. And but a few short years ago, nor could I. "They shall be in charge of themselves, if they succeed."

"But Sir John will not let that happen, will he, Mama? Didn't the king send his men to help Sir John, Papa, and the others fight those bad men?"

"Yes, Mathias, he did."

"When do we get to go back home?"

It is only now that I realize my children still believe we are going back. "We are not."

Instantly, Mathias and Ruby look at me, bewildered. "But why cannot we go back home, Mama?" he says, now unable to control his tears.

"We are no longer welcome, Mathias. Our neighbours want something we do not believe is right, and so we go to where the king will give us a new home and protection." I reach to wipe the tears from his soft cheeks.

"Our neighbours might not be happy if we stayed?" He is beginning to make connections to our situation, and the men we met on the trail. So that he might understand the truth, I put both hands on his face and I look him directly in the eye. "No, Mathias. They would not."

"Bad men scary, Mama. I scared." Scurrying to my lap, Jacob once again buries his head in my neck and cries, desperately grabbing at me to comfort him. As I put both arms around him, I look toward my poor, sweet Ruby, sitting on the cold ground, crying uncontrollably, holding her knees tight to her, rocking back and forth repeating softly through sobs, "Oh, Dolly, oh, Dolly." The finality of our life in Johnstown is most pitifully evident. I could easily join these little ones in their desperate heartbreak, for it dwells in me, but I have a duty to them greater than my own need for mourning the life we knew. I try and revive them, giving each some water before we continue on with our day's march. "It will be okay, children. Your papa waits for us in the king's lands. He has gone ahead with Sir John to get our new home ready."

"Who will look after our farm?" Mathias cannot let go of what he believes waits for us still.

"Only the house stands — remember?"

"Where da horsey, Mama?"

"Gone, Jacob." It seems there is little I can do, after so much to contemplate, that will help them see hope where none may exist.

We have all stayed in silence throughout this long afternoon, I suppose partly from reflecting on the good fortune at having survived the morning raid, and partly from the exhaustion after these many days we have travelled. Jacob sleeps easily once again upon my shoulder; sleep is a wonderful state, though I do not take much comfort in it, for it leaves us most vulnerable. The lack of rest, combined with my constant malaise, has left a troublesome feeling hanging over me. I pray I will rally and find that my fears are for naught . . . yet something within warns that I do not fear in vain.

Lost in thought, I almost scream when Elizabeth grabs my hand gently. "I am sorry, dear friend, to scare you. Are you okay?"

"Yes, of course."

"Are you sure? You are drenched with sweat, dear, and the day does not warrant it."

It is only now, with Elizabeth's mention of it, that I realize my clothes are sticking to my body, with the effects of what I can only assume is a fever brought on by the distress. My lightheaded state has allowed for some relief from reality, but in allowing this, I consider I tread in dangerous territory, similar to the one that Annabel Burnhart crossed into but a day ago. Feeling the full effects of my illness, I swoon. Elizabeth catches Jacob just as he falls from my arms, and as she does so, she calls to Mr. VanAllen, "We must rest!"

I do not know how long I have slept, but as I regain my senses, I realize it is dark. Panicking, I look about to see where my precious ones are. With a touch on the arm, I turn to see my friend Elizabeth, who lies by my side and whispers, "They are fine. They have eaten a meal and have slept well these many hours." Assured of their safety, I realize that while I am yet feeling unwell, I do not feel flushed as before.

"What happened?"

"You were in need of rest, dear friend." I lay my head back upon the ground, as the exertion of sitting upright, such a simple task, leaves me shaky. "Here, have some water. And you must eat tonight."

From her manner of voice, I feel my friend is as a mother speaking to a child. No protestations will have her relent. I take the cup of water and find I am very thirsty, and happy to have my cup refilled twice.

It has been many days since I have partaken of so much. Tonight my will for conserving such precious resources cannot be matched by my body's need for it. But when Elizabeth hands me some bannock and salted meat that she has rationed from her own supply to sustain the children, at this I draw the line. "I will only have bannock."

"Yes, you will, and this meat."

"No, I must not; it is for the little ones."

"Exactly," she says, handing it to me. I meet her gaze and feel less alone with my ill-guarded secret. Emotion begins to rise in me, but I cannot let it out, for I am sure I will lose all hope . . . and now, more than ever, this is what keeps me going.

After my small meal, I lay my head back down and look up to the stars, the same stars that just the night before welcomed Annabel into their care. Despite the peace in this thought, I know these stars will not welcome me this night. I feel the nourishment shoring up my strength, and in reflecting on the horrors I have seen this day, I know my unwavering determination is intact. As I listen to the now familiar howls and sounds of animals that come to life at night, I feel myself begin to give into sleep. With the haunting sound of a loon calling its mate in the dark, I hold my hope protectively with my hands and bargain with the silence within, "We have come this far. Hold on, we are almost there."

CHAPTER 26

In spite of the nearly full moon shining brightly upon us, this night is grim as the pain becomes unbearable. I must stifle my urge to make any sound, for the little ones sleep nearby. I have not been able to rest these many days and struggle upon the journey. My friend has secured the help of Mr. Burnhart to carry Jacob, as my protests waned with the reality that I was no longer capable of doing so. I was grateful for the aid. Thinking Mr. Burnhart cold at one time, his care for his dear Annabel showed a sympathetic nature. It was evident that he understood the situation more than my sensibilities wished for, but this had long gone beyond any choice. In these wild places, there is no choice; no standing on propriety; we are most exposed in our current circumstances, and I am utterly laid bare.

Understanding what is to be, I tug on Elizabeth's shawl, as she lay closer to me, in preparation for what we both understand must be. "I will watch over them; please take my prayers with you, dear friend." I can see tears running down her face, by the few flames in our small, dying fire. I cannot cry, for this is what it is. Looking over them, one, two, three, I commit to their safe arrival into their father's arms.

I stumble as I make my way into the dark forest along a path shrouded in mist. With only a hint of moonlight through the canopy providing any light, I grab branches and trees for support when taken by the pain. Overcome with the strong smell of pine as I break branches in my effort to remain standing, I cannot help but retch and heave—this, too, a familiar part of our journey. A dreadful knowing, which has been buried within me, has now stripped away all defence—exposing me—and now I must endure all . . . feel all.

I continue, venturing just far enough to muffle any noise that might be made. Finding a clearing, on what I now see clearly by the light of the moon is the edge of the mountain, I set myself upon a soft patch of grass, with only my shawl providing any warmth on this chilly night. The secret I have kept through these dark days, the last faint hope of new life to provide deliverance from this fearful time, is not to be. I can only accept this and do what must be done.

I sit among the trees, whose boughs bend and sway with the breeze, making a soft, comforting sound — not the silence that forces one to listen for the breaking of branches, the howls of beasts searching for their prey, or, even more frightful, no sound, which signals an unnatural way for this wilderness. I am glad for the sounds that fill the air, and in this short reprieve, the pain has quieted, the movement has quieted, and I am able to look about this chosen ground.

Are the mists, which now envelop me, angels' breath upon the cool air creating another place, unknown to all but mine own and me? This will be our world together — the only one we will ever know — guarded in the arms of this protected place and time. I feel the arrival begin, and though I might want to fight it, do not, for I know within my soul this will come to pass . . . not to be undone by man . . . this is God's will, and we are in his care.

The pain is unbearable . . . though I must bear it. "Oh, Lord, please deliver us from this place, this time. Oh, Lord!" I throw the shawl from my shoulders, as sweat beads my forehead. The will I must exert not to yell out is all-consuming. Even the pain I now feel in the babe's arrival is no equal for my soul crying out. I am sure I am dying — that something beyond the babe's making its way into this sickened world is dying. Laying my shawl upon the ground in front of me, so that this poor creature might have some comfort if born alive, I push through the final gripping pain.

Silence.

I am afraid to look. I have never seen a babe born at such an early time, not but six months along. Would it look at all like a babe, as had my others, now sleeping soundly? Sensing some movement and the faintest sound, I bring myself to look beyond my skirt. There, lying with eyes wide open, is the smallest babe I have ever laid eyes upon. With no hope of her survival, I cannot let her linger upon my shawl.

I wrap her tightly, and lift her to me.

Hearing a noise in the woods behind me, I fear not, for I know it is my dearest friend, Elizabeth, come to watch over me . . . and my precious one. I look upon her delicate features as she looks upon me. In the moonlight shrouded by the mist of our world, I see that, though small, she has the very look of an Eamer. A daughter my Peter would have looked upon with pride. She does not cry, nor does she try to suckle as my others had. I know there is no need to try. This time is a gift . . . a small mercy in such a dark time. To see her breathe the air of the world, to look upon the face of her mother and to receive my comfort is by the very mercy of God. I cannot help but cry now for our most precious time together—so unexpected. Staring at each other, I smile at her, wanting her to remember the happiness she has brought to the world, if only to my world. "Dear God, bless this child whom I soon commit to your care. I name her Maria Catrina Eamer, as she is part of my own soul, and thus is taken part of it with her." I pour a sprinkle of water from my canteen to baptize the babe, my baby . . . *mine own.*

Looking down at her in my arms, I keep my eyes fixed on my delicate, fleeting little one as life slowly slips away; taking in every movement of her little chest rising and falling, and silently holding the gaze of one another in a knowing between us. I hum the melody so oft heard by my children as they were lulled to sleep. Then, in too little a time, in my loving arms, her eyes flicker, and life fades.

Silence.

"Let me take her now, dear friend." Elizabeth quietly emerges from the woods, but I cannot let her—lying silently, serenely in my arms—be put to rest by anyone else. It is my duty as her mother to do so.

CHAPTER 27

I have lost my most secret, intimate companion; though fragile and fleeting, her absence marks my heart most profoundly. The depth of my loneliness and despair makes me most violently ill. My only comfort is the memory of our time together and the image of her sweet face that haunts my dreams by night and remains always in my mind when I am awake.

Upon our journey this day, but a few since that fateful night, my three little ones continue with their usual wonder and innocence. Elizabeth keeps a close watch on them with her own in her arms; and she watches me as well. The ever-pensive Mr. Burnhart has taken a special interest in our care, and though he remains silent most days, he always carries my Jacob. There is relief in this, and I allow myself to spend time with "mine own."

I see her even now; feel her in my arms. I could not bear to put her down, but as the first hints of pink and orange appeared upon the horizon, I knew our time had drawn to an end. I laid her upon the soft grass that had greeted her when entering this world. Still and beautifully at peace, I yearned to join her in the stillness. For a brief moment, I envied her return to the Father, and the protection of His kingdom, but my sole duty is to deliver the three little ones entrusted to me safely to their father and their destinies. I, too, may find comfort in Peter's arms once again, though a part of me will always remain in this place.

Pulling the kerchief from my bodice, where I had kept it close to me along this journey, I unfolded it, exposing the delicate content. I set the petal, my proof of life's enduring hope, upon the still heart of mine own, wrapped in my shawl much as I had wrapped her brothers and sister. Slowly I pulled back the grass beside her and gathered a rock to help create a cradle to set her in. The mind plays tricks and lies to us, it seems — for unless I thought of it as a cradle, I could not have borne the grief that was ready to consume me.

Once the cradle was prepared, I leaned over her and kissed her still warm face, studying the delicate nature of her form, as I had the flower laid upon her. Though the glow of the moon had afforded each of us a time to look upon the other's face, the earliest morning light allowed me to study her so as to commit her to memory. I knew she was to be mine — and mine alone — for in not knowing of her, Peter would never feel as I now do.

Swaddling her tightly, I pulled the shawl over her face, never to look upon her again, yet knowing she would never leave me. I covered the place where she was now at her rest, and once the grass returned to where it had been, the site looked as though little had changed . . . yet all had. The mists that had set upon us in the night began to rise ever higher, swirling about and fading into the brightening morning sky; and I understood mine own, my daughter, Maria Catrina — for she had a name in life — departed with them to rejoin the realm of the angels.

Looking up toward the horizon, the sliver of sun, which in a flash appeared upon the mountain ridge, broke the trance and day began again. The warmth it brought reminded me that life continued — though I might not want it to — and brought me back to another time. *My tree was now beginning to bear fruit*, I thought, smiling to myself . . . and then the realization struck me down. I lay upon the grass and wept as the sun rose upon what was left of me in my barren state.

CHAPTER 28

Unsure now how many days we have travelled, I have been wrapped in a haze of what was; what is; what is to come. I have felt out of time, simply existing, but slowly, moments of simple pleasures are returning. Ruby has befriended young Mary Burnhart, the once sallow-eyed girl. Her cheeks, now pink with the freshness of the air, signal she, too, is coming back to life. Her raven hair and my Ruby's yellow locks tumble about their faces in natural ringlets as they skip silently hand-in-hand. Understanding not to sing aloud, they nevertheless enjoy their time together, seemingly being in tune with the songs in their minds, which give them great pleasure. It is hard to stifle a smile at their customary ways, held in such contrast against the backdrop of the dire situation we are in. Somehow, youthful spirit prevails despite all that has transpired. Even Mathias is slowly relinquishing his role as protector and finds companionship with the two younger Burnhart boys, Lucas and Isaiah. As boys are evidently more inhibited with one another, I observe Mathias working hard to be seen as grown-up beyond his years in the eyes of his companions. They walk about, admiring the natural landscape, pointing at objects of interest with the walking sticks they carry, and nodding when something is of particular importance. But they, too, always stay silent. Though it has been of particular concern how we should keep ones so young from making noise, our journey had proven that even those who are very young have the capacity to understand survival.

Elizabeth, often carrying Isabel to keep pace, has stayed close since my daughter had come and left this world. We pass our days in silent companionship. Jacob is again hoisted upon my hip as I regain strength to carry him once more. Mr. Burnhart, having carried him for a number of days, has relinquished his care back to me. He now walks with his oldest son, Thomas, but nine years old and a trusted companion to his father. I take note as he studies his children, and wonder if their resemblance to his wife provides some comfort to this stoic man. Only upon the night he lost Annabel did I see him shed a tear; otherwise, while kindness has revealed itself, he has reverted to being a quiet, if less brooding, man.

Entering the foothills on the other side of the mountains, there is a sense that our days upon the journey come to an end. Our Mohawk guide has not visited us in two days, and as this does not seem to alarm Mr. VanAllen, we understand it is an expected event. We share what food is left among us, and the few rabbits he brought upon his last day have been rationed by Mr. VanAllen. The trees change from those of pine forests to ones of white birch with early season light green leaves flicking about in the breezes. While dense, these forests are not as dark as those on our journey, and though no words have been spoken on the matter, there is a palpable change in the level of concern among our group, and a sense of being within the territory of friends once again.

Upon the end of our third day in the foothills, Mr. VanAllen sets about lighting the customary nightly fire and suddenly announces, "We have reached the protection of Quebec." I look at Elizabeth in surprise. We were not greeted by anyone as expected. Before we can speak, Mr. Burnhart asks, "And where are the people who wait for these women and children?" He seems to understand that, even though we have survived our journey thus far, we will need the protection of our men once in our new homeland.

"They will be greeted in Montreal by the authorities, and after they are delivered safely, are no longer any of my concern." It is evident we have not penetrated the affections of Mr. VanAllen in any way.

"And when, sir, might we reach Montreal?"

"Two days, *if* we keep our pace." His voice gives warning that we had better keep it as he wishes. It is evident that we are but a commission.

Despite Mr. VanAllen's announcing the previous night that we are in

Quebec, the land looks no different than it had the days since we have moved into the foothills; only that we are told so do I know we are in the king's lands. But now on the high ground of a clearing, we emerge from the forest, and a great valley comes into view. I feel as though I am dreaming, for the valley I now look upon — vast and stretching to the horizon — is cut by a silvery ribbon, and I should believe it to be our own home valley, if the wear of body and soul did not remind me so acutely of the truth.

While two days of travel are yet ahead of us, we are renewed by the thought of meeting our loved ones again. In my heart, I know we are not assured of this coming to pass — much has happened — but somehow I feel sure I should see Peter again; that he should hold his children in his arms again . . . those who have made it to the end of our exodus. But, where we are renewed with some hope, Elizabeth becomes pensive in our last days. In unknown lands, full of unknown people, Elizabeth does not know who, or what, awaits her and her small child. As we continue soaking in the sun and awe-inspiring view, I reach for Elizabeth's hand, and with a silent reassurance — as it is my turn — I hold her hand tight as a promise that she will not be left alone.

CHAPTER 29

Today we make for Montreal.

We knew we rested near the banks of the silver river, seen from the crest of the foothills of two days ago, for throughout the previous evening we could hear the gathering of geese upon the safety of the river for the night. Their sounds, familiar and comforting, lulled us into our slumber, though my dreams are yet haunted by a tiny face.

This last morning of our exodus, for now I am able to come to terms with the weight of such a word, of such an experience, greets us with the usual warmth of a late spring day. As I look up at the overcast sky with just a hint of sun breaking through the clouds in vibrant bursts of light, I reflect on what might await us. While it holds the promise of a new day, when once we moved ever one day closer to Peter, we were aware of what each day would likely bring, walking one step more upon an unknown path; but this day I cannot yet know what it holds for us. Knowing this to be our last day, I feel the exhaustion of body and spirit. The ebbing of my strength and determination leaves me in a disheartened state and I must now make my way to Peter, my true home, which I pray now lies but across the shore. Even in my hope for one whom I have not gazed upon in many weeks, I feel not all of me shall greet him; part of my fragmented soul shall always rest upon the ridge of a mountain wrapped in a grey shawl. I shall forever long for what cannot be — for who cannot be. Though the world warms with the sun, I am cold; guarded in what I will allow myself to feel and remember, yet hoping I will feel again, as I once did.

We have walked for a number of hours, and as we approach the shore, we can see the silhouette of dwellings come into view upon the horizon. A long line of structures, and the spires of great places of worship, is set in front of a large hill, which stands oddly disconnected from any mountains. This foreign landscape, and structures of such a number as I have never in my life laid eyes upon, does not fill my heart with the relief or anticipation at what it may hold, but rather apprehension, as the images of my old home dissipate. It seems my mind had led me to believe that we would rediscover our old home in new lands, and this falsity gave strength to keep moving forward. Hope is ever around the corner, given and taken in such abundance these past years that I should scold myself for hoping that Peter will meet us upon these unknown shores . . . and yet, I do hope.

Great ships are tied upon the opposite bank, and we can see one, with sails billowing in full view down the river, making its way to our own destination. With confidence that we are in a protected place at last, we walk along the river's bank. I seemingly begin to bear the full weight of what we have been through and what yet awaits. Even with this overwhelming apprehension — exhaustion — I smile while our children talk excitedly of the adventures to come once we cross to the other shore. The boys, having run to the water's edge to look for fish in the river, begin to search for sticks they expect to fashion into fishing poles. Mathias looks much altered. I can see the veil of worry lift, and innocence return to my boy.

Among the most beautiful of sounds are the voices of Ruby and Mary, who sing aloud the songs that once only existed in their minds. For the first time, we are reassured that we have safeguarded their youthful spirit. I even allow Jacob to amble about along the shoreline with Isabel, and though they stumble about, they have found their footing to walk on their own. In these last moments upon this side of the shore, Elizabeth and I interlock arms and hold on, not knowing if we shall ever feel the comfort of our most trusted and intimate friendship again. I cannot help but think that she knows more of who I now am than Peter does; that she is one who can truly understand the sacrifices made upon our journey.

The light of the day begins to fade, and as the sky becomes a brilliant, fiery orange, it reflects on the fast-moving water, the geese settling upon the safety of the river once again. The safety of the river:

Perhaps it will signal this for us, as well, I pray. We make our way to a point on the shore where we presume a scow awaits our arrival, we presume, as we see a hand wave in our direction. Mr. VanAllen greets the man genially, which is a surprise to us, for we have not seen him smile before; yet when he looks back at us, there is no evidence of kindness, and his eyes remain dark and full of disdain. A number of paces ahead of us now, this man raises his voice to be heard over the rushing water. "They are a haggard-looking lot, but were we not expecting more?"

"Well, I did what I could, but not all can handle the journey, as you well know." Mr. VanAllen is cruel in his manner of speaking.

"Well, we'll take who we have across and hope you get full payment for their safe arrival." These men seem unconcerned that we—and in particular, Mr. Burnhart—can hear them speak of us as though we are chattels.

Seated upon the floor of the scow, we move away from the shore, and I look across the river.

"What river do we cross?" asks Mr. Burnhart of our boatman.

"This is the mighty St. Lawrence River, sir, running from the ocean to many miles inland."

As he regales Mr. Burnhart with river stories, I do not listen, for I am looking at the shore toward which we head and I can now see the forms of people coming into view. As we slowly move closer, our boatman seems to work hard against the strong current. Approaching the shore, the hill, which seems out of place in the flat landscape, now begins to loom over us, and the buildings are more sizable than I had imagined from far across the river. It is hard not to be astounded by such a sight, for I have never seen such dwellings, which stretch along the shore until they disappear upon the horizon in either direction. We come from places along the edges of civilization; places where communities are small and all are known to us. I should not imagine this is true in this great place.

I slowly begin to see the faces of some of the men, and the uniforms they wear. If he lives, Peter will be among them. The look of desperation on their faces tells me they wait for loved ones expected, but who have not yet arrived. By their numbers, many will leave disappointed.

Seeing the faces of these men, full of anticipation, I know that with all we have experienced, the full price paid for freedom will be steep for many, as it has been for us.

Even as the boat moves closer to what may be our salvation, I cannot help but take my eyes off the men of the king's forces and look back at the growing distance to the shore we have just left. The tears, which flow freely, are for what I leave behind. Finally, I turn back and can now make out Peter's face as he steps from the crowd, and by his expression of relief, I know he can see me and his children. Seeing the joy on his face, I decide that I shall not burden him with the truth of our sacrifice, as he has no knowledge of her; and so she shall always remain mine own.

CHAPTER 30

Reaching the shore, the boatman pulls the scow alongside one of the king's ships in port. We are insignificant compared to the majestic size of this beautiful ship. When he used the term "haggard" to describe us, it seems our boatman had not been wrong. In contrast to the opulence of the ships, buildings, and people waiting upon the shore, we were shells of people. The dignity we once possessed had been lost upon our perilous journey.

Before the scow is secured by the ropes thrown to shore, Mr. VanAllen leaps off, not waiting to aid us. His job done, he immediately makes for the first commissioned officer he finds, demanding, "Who do I see about payment?" As he disappears into the crowd, I see him meet a friend who grabs him about the shoulders, greeting him in genuine friendship, saying, "Time for a drink, then, Josiah?" It was the first and only time I was to hear that this hard man, commissioned with our safe arrival to Montreal, had a Christian name, even if it seems the only thing Christian about him.

Disembarking, Peter runs to us with an exuberance I had not expected. He seems the same man who had left us in the night many weeks before, yet cuts a distinguished and unfamiliar figure in his uniform. Finally releasing me, his children still clinging to his legs, we look into each other's eyes. It is instantly understood between us that the relief in once again finding each other will not undo what has happened. With a timid, knowing smile — that little can be expressed of this nightmare we have endured — he simply says, "I knew my children would be safe with you, my dear. You are a brave and valiant mother."

Proceeding to register within the colony, the chaos of the scene is disconcerting and makes it difficult to see where our travel companions have gone. As I look around to find Elizabeth and Isabel, I am seized by the arm and turn to see Mr. Burnhart. "It has been my great pleasure to have made your acquaintance, Mrs. Eamer." With a genial bow to me and my husband, this man, having been privy to the most raw experiences of the human condition, leaves us as dignified as he had met us, though he is forever changed. Mounting a waiting carriage with his four children, they depart to continue their lives.

Once within the small building that serves as the registration site, I see Elizabeth ahead of us, Isabel in her arms. Even though we were the only ones on our travels, the room is crowded with the king's men receiving orders and, I suspect, making arrangements for their own families. I hear Elizabeth give her name to the soldier who sits behind the table with papers strewn about, and as he looks through lists of names, the walls and roof of this tiny building make me feel trapped. We have slept under the stars in shelters made of tree boughs for many nights, and now being inside a structure such as this makes it hard to breathe. The overpowering smell of the oil from the lantern, now lit to create some light, catches in my throat and chokes me with its stinging odour.

"Ah, here you are, Elizabeth Hartle," the soldier says matter-of-factly, as he ticks her off his list. He continues to fill out some paperwork, only looking up to ask the full name of her child, "Isabel Anna Hartle." I see her embrace Isabel tighter as she speaks her name, and though she sleeps upon her mother's shoulder, I notice her wince with the tightening. He hands my dearest friend the paper, and says that she is to wait until someone comes for her. "You may sit along the side on one of the chairs until then." He is abrupt and gives little thought to her dire state. I see her pick up her paper, and as she passes by me, I look down to see the reason she has tightened her grip on her child — she is the only family she has in this place; a notation made on her paper stands out among all others: "Widow."

We have only one more person in front of us before we may register. I look over at my friend, sitting in stunned silence, looking utterly lost. She is adrift in this new life. I realize how desperate the situation has become for Elizabeth and Isabel, perhaps even more so than on the trails, for there we had each other, though I was more reliant on her. I want to run and comfort her, but we are once again in our customary roles, I as mother and wife, and Peter once again our protector. As I continue to look over at this most pitiful scene, I notice Elizabeth looks toward the door that now creaks open, and in a sudden, desperate yell, she calls out, "Mama!" Her mother runs to embrace her and her waking child, without the restraint generally expected. Strong though she may have been on our journey, I now clearly understand just how young this girl is in the arms of her mother.

Moving forward as our turn arrives to register our family, I look back to see Elizabeth walking, supported by her mother, as her father carries his granddaughter to the door. I am desperate to call to her; to bid her well; I pray a silent prayer that the Lord should afford us occasion to meet in happier times. Just as I am about to turn to face the soldier at the table, Elizabeth looks back over her shoulder, tears streaming down her face, and in memories all our own, we understand what we have meant to each other.

The soldier who is to make our arrival in this new land official asks, "How long have you travelled?" I do not know the answer to this simple question, for the number of days matter little in what seems a lifetime. I am surprised by Peter's voice answering, "Twenty-one days."

Looking down at the paper handed to me I cannot believe the word that accompanies my own name: "Refugee."

CHAPTER 31

We are afforded little comfort in this new land, although I am grateful for what the king provides. Our shelter among those who have come from our home territory is a tent in a makeshift community. It is muddy with the rain, and cold at night, but we do not complain, as it is comfort we have not had in days. Many speak with the common voice of our people, though I do not know any of them, except our men. My own family and my husband's kin are yet journeying, they say, and I watch as my father-in-law and brothers wait by the shoreline, as Peter did but a few days ago. With every passing sunrise and sunset, hope is strained and takes a most distressing toll on them. Their faces are drawn, with blackened eyes from lack of sleep, and it is difficult to look upon such helplessness, for I know too intimately what they feel. I cannot allow myself to tread in those places within me, for the shred of soul that remains in this place will be extinguished by it.

"Any news yet, dear brother?" Peter's voice is tinged with pity as Martin passes by on his daily walk to the shoreline to await those who may yet come.

"No, we expect them any day. They say large groups such as theirs sometime take longer to arrive." He glances at me, smiling weakly, as I keep the children occupied in our tent. By his voice it is evident he fully understands what this delay may signal and takes hope in what little conjecture is made.

"Dear sister, I hope you are well? We surely rejoice in your safe arrival."

"We are well, Martin. Please take our prayers with you." I do not smile or offer reassurance, as I believe he hopes for; I know too well the dangers that lurk upon the trails and can only rely on my faith in

God to deliver them all to us.

"Shall I go with you, then?" While Peter has often expressed his great relief at our safe arrival these few days, it is obvious he feels guilt in doing so while his mother and sisters travel. "No, you must attend to your own family, Peter. There is little to do but wait."

Watching as Martin, standing tall as ever, moves to meet his father and brothers waiting for him along the path, I note that his stride is urgent; and though he may be rushing only to endure hours of helpless, hopeful anticipation—dashed these many days—he happily does so if it somehow brings him the news he seeks.

There is little to do in this place, though I mend what clothes Peter has need of with the few provisions we are allotted. Starting a small fire on which to boil the meat and potatoes we have been given, Mathias, yet my aide, helps to pile the wood upon the makeshift hearth, while Peter sets it alight. They work in concert once more, and Mathias delights in it, but Peter is far away in his thoughts, his furrowed brow indicating his worry.

"I must travel to the port to inquire about plans for our settlement. I shall return soon."

Knowing we are safe in this place, I understand his need to wait along with his kin, and do not question his motives but simply nod and smile. He rushes to his father's side and takes his place among them, as they walk, as always, shoulder to shoulder.

"Mama?"

"Yes, my dear?"

"Is Mary's mama gone?"

"Yes, she is gone."

It is dreadful the things my children know to be true about this world. At three, Ruby should not think upon such appalling memories, nor understand what these mean, but in a camp full of forlorn families, not all whole—some missing mothers, many missing fathers— it is impossible, I think, for little ones not to ponder such changed circumstances.

"Her papa will sing to her at night?"

"Yes, dearest, her papa will sing to her." Ruby seems pleased with my answer, for such customs are important to ones so young. The comforting sound of their parent's voice lulling them to sleep brings reassurance that all is well in their little world, even as the world around them is full of chaos and madness.

"Mama?"

"Yes, Ruby?"

"I miss my friend." Her eyes well with tears, though she remains stoic, a trait I hope comes from her father's sensibility and not from the damage that might have been caused on our exodus. I know the truth . . . I understand the pain caused by their parting. With so much happiness taken from her, discovering another soul in such dire circumstances must create kinship — does create kinship — in knowing so intimately the burdens the other bears. I often think of my own friend Elizabeth, and hope she has found a place in this land. The last news we had was that she had moved to the camp at Vercheres, where many of her own people have gone. I think I shall never see her again, and cannot offer any hope to Ruby, so I shall offer what I can. Setting my sewing upon the cot, I pick her up and place her upon my lap. Holding her tight to me, I whisper in her ear, "We shall have one another, my Ruby, and someday we will make new friends." She nuzzles into my shoulder, as she had just a few years before, and takes comfort in her mama's arms; and I take comfort in hers.

As music strikes up in the camp, I jump at the intrusion in the silence and look for the source of the sound: a fiddle that resonates in the still night air. While a cheerful tune, it is frightfully loud. Though our life is no longer shrouded in silence, our existence allowed to be known, I am yet apprehensive with the usual, everyday life going on about me. As others gather around the man who plays, I relax and realize we need not hush . . . and may enjoy it.

Peter returned at dusk, and I did not require news; their gait, even from afar, was evidence enough to know we wait still. Sitting by the firelight, our Jacob and Ruby sleep soundly in the safety of our tent, while Mathias, enjoying his time by our side, looks ever upon his father's face, as though he should wake from a dream and find him not there. He seems utterly mesmerized to have found him, and where this should bring me happiness, as it does Mathias, it pains me that he should have feared the loss at all. I feel most acutely the burden of what we have experienced. With my mind relinquishing the need for survival, I am now tortured by reflecting on what we have all endured these many days . . . and years.

It is five days since our arrival, and remembering the arduous nature of the journey, I realize that the endurance it demands of our people yet in the wilds must surely be unbearable. I imagine our loved ones in the dark, looking at the same stars I now see in the sky, and cannot help but think of Annabel . . . I pray her fate has not befallen them. I see the faces of my own family, and wonder if my father has survived his imprisonment or if he yet suffers under the brutality of the rebels. He and my dear mother surely do not travel with my brothers and sisters, and I wonder how they shall find us once again. I gasp out loud at the thought.

"Catrina, are you well?" Peter rushes to my side and catches me as I falter upon the bench.

"I am well, just a little tired."

"Mathias, please go to bed now. I believe Mama will join you."

"No, no. I should like to enjoy the evening with you, my dear."

He looks at me with concern, but relents as I smile in reassurance of my wellness.

"Mathias, 'tis very late. We shall be in soon," I promise.

"Good night, Mama. Good night, Papa." He hesitates, and I understand he is not used to being so far from me when he sleeps.

"I shall put you to bed, dearest." I turn to Peter, who watches our interaction most intently, seeming to sense Mathias's apprehension.

"Son, come here, please." Mathias, surprised by his father's request, turns and dutifully stands before him. "You are a brave boy. I am very proud of how you took my stead upon your journey. Good night and rest well. You are safe under my protection once again—I promise." Pulling Mathias to him, Peter embraces him most tenderly, and I see his lip quiver as he holds tight. Struggling to control what I can only surmise is guilt and a rush of fear of losing this precious one, Mathias wraps his arms around his papa's neck ever tighter and lays his head upon his shoulder, enjoying the reassurance of his father's arms. Finally setting him back to rights, Peter, composed in his usual manner once more, bids Mathias good night.

Pulling back the warm blanket to allow Mathias to slip into the cot without disturbing Ruby and Jacob, I kiss him on his soft cheeks and look down upon his sleepy face. "You are tired, my little one. Sleep well."

"Mama, I am not little," he says with some indignation.

"You are right. You are a big boy now, and Mama should remember this."

As I turn to leave, he grabs my hand. "Where are you going?"

"Just to speak with your papa by the fire. I will not be but a few feet from you."

"Might you leave the flap open so that I can see you?"

"Yes, I will leave it open."

"Mama?" He hesitates.

"Yes."

"Will you sing to me?"

I move to kneel at his side and with a soft, whispered voice begin singing the melody that has always provided solace, even upon dark trails. Soon his eyes slowly close, and he sleeps. Before turning to rejoin Peter, I count them as always: one, two, three . . . they are safe. Exiting the tent, I look at the stars dancing about high above me and offer a silent: "Good night, my sweet . . . mine own."

I take my place upon the bench once more. Peter pokes the fire with a stick, making the embers fly into the sky, spark, and quickly die out as they float off in the air. The mix of music and hushed conversations within the camp creates a sense of comfort, even in such surroundings. Peter tentatively looks at me, knowing there are experiences we no longer share. Ours is an unnatural silence. He has not asked me about my journey, and I shall not offer any details, in an unspoken understanding that what has been shall be left upon the trail.

CHAPTER 32

From our vantage point, I see the many ships that ply this river. I wonder from what far-off places these have come, and where they might yet go. I often watch the sails as they move ever farther away, and then most suddenly slip from the horizon as though they never existed at all. Commerce abounds in this busy community, and even as our people, and so many others, are without assurance of their safe arrival here, life goes on. We, it seems, have become part of this commerce. Men are hired to bring us to these shores, men are charged with our registration; we are outfitted with supplies and set up in these "refugee camps" with provisions coming to us daily for our sustenance. It seems we drive much of this economy. It is a life we have not known, and I long for our simple ways.

We are eight days arrived, and word is that many yet travel the trails to make their way here. Hope is our only mercy, for each day the time seems to grow longer, the pain of the wait unbearable. Though many thankfully come to these shores daily, they are haggard from the perilous journey. Only now do I realize how pitiful we must have appeared to those who waited for us. Vacant stares of distress and bewilderment on each face leave little doubt as to who are the new arrivals. Some of our neighbours have made it to our camp, but we have not yet had occasion to speak to them, as they settle in.

Our life here, which I pray will be most temporary, begins to find a new order. Many of the customs from home, such as our meals and prayers together, are practised with less comfort than before, but the absence of fear makes us rejoice in them.

Jacob, boundless in his energy, occupies the efforts of Ruby and Mathias in ensuring his care, and often safety, within the camp. There is little to entertain the children, and they yearn to make friends. Many do not allow their children to roam freely. It is understandable, since we are strangers to one another and do not yet know this place and its ways. My need to have the children ever under my watchful eye is a fixation I bring with me from the journey — one of the many scars I feel upon my soul. Perhaps in time I shall allow them the freedom to flourish and not burden them with the unease that is ever my companion.

Preparing the midday meal, I hear a group approaching from behind and am brought to my knees in thankfulness to see the smiles upon the faces of our men. Carrying provisions for their families, I see glimpses of my mother-in-law, sisters, and their children. I pray I shall see them all, for I cannot yet take account of how many have survived. As Peter comes to us, we watch as our kin move to their own tents down the row from where we are. Though they have the familiar despondent look of many travellers, they are all here. Even now, there is hope we may be able to rebuild our lives together. With optimism filling me in such abundance, my heart pounds within my breast as I look to see if more are coming.

"Are my mother, father, brothers, and sisters among those who have arrived, Peter?"

His smile dissipates as he looks at me, knowing what I seek in the distance. "No, my dear. There are no more arrivals yet." With my hopes dashed, I cry inconsolably. The relief of finding so many coming back to us is mixed with such bitterness that my own kin should not be among them. I am wholly unable to contain myself and remain upon the ground crying, caring little who sees me. The children run to my side, but this time, I have no need to gather myself, and Peter sets them upon the bench to await their meal, as he ushers me into our tent. "Lie down and rest, my dear. Surely we will have news soon. I promise I shall wait upon the shore daily until we know." Exhausted by despair, I feel myself give in to sleep, caressing a hope that is no longer there . . .

I wake in the late evening to the sounds of the geese coming to take their rest upon the safety of the river for the night. The camp is quieting for the day, and the familiar murmur of quiet conversations signal that all are settling in for the night; no more are expected this day. Though a hint of daylight is yet evident in the brilliant glow of orange upon the horizon, I do not rise. I watch as Peter tends to his children as in my customary way, and seeing that they delight in his company, and he in theirs, I turn once again to dream of mine own.

CHAPTER 33

With the early light of day greeting the sun as it crests above the horizon, much of our day's labour must be done while the heat is yet at bay, for we swelter by midday and must take refuge in the shade of our tents, which are now set under the canopy of the trees to provide further relief.

These four weeks since our arrival have been a trial I hope will soon come to an end. Our camp is not permanent, and we simply await new arrangements. We are a displaced people, and in our numbers it seems the rebels shall win their freedom. Those who arrive now are most often moved on to other camps that have been established to accommodate long stays. I should not wish this for us, and Peter and his kin work hard to find alternative arrangements. It is only because he has fought with Sir John that we are afforded the comfort of staying here until this may occur.

The heat and strain of the season has taken many from us. Disease is rife, and takes children and the infirm with it. Only one tragedy similar to mine has played out, and I was glad my mother-in-law attended to the poor soul. I envied her, for she was able to join her precious one in the afterlife, and I am left behind to suffer the knowledge of my loss. There is yet a day I do not think of her . . . I feel most grateful for those who have survived, but am torn between my wish for both life and death. I trust God has spared me for a reason, and I will endeavour to be ever thankful by doing His good work on this earth. A makeshift burial site has been established a short distance from the camp. It seems so pitiful that they should arrive in this promised land only to be buried in it. I pray they took some comfort in the knowledge that here they were free again.

Peter left before the light of morning, and now as night approaches, he returns from the shoreline with a letter in hand, though it is not this I focus on. His stride is determined, and he, along with many of our camp, once again wears a uniform. Accompanied by his father and brothers, I know they have been called to continue to fight. My gentle men are now soldiers in the employ of the king, and though they fight under Sir John, I have seen the work that is to be done and am yet sorry for it, though it saved us.

I go about making his evening meal and do not speak. Noticing my discontent at the thought of his leaving again, he does not hesitate to announce: "I have joined Sir John's Second Battalion, which he has just raised. Many in camp who fought as militia have enlisted." I look around and see the faces of the many women being told as I am now, that our men are to put themselves in harm's way once again. "It is the only form of gratitude we might show for all that has been done for us." He seems resigned that he should shoulder the brunt of the burden for our safe arrival . . . he does not know the price he has truly paid.

"This has just come." Handing me the letter, I sit upon the bench and slowly open it, dreading that it might contain dire news. Sensing my apprehension, Peter says, " 'Tis good news, my dear. Read it."

September 24, 1780

Dear Sister:

These three weeks we have been in camp at Chambly along the Richelieu River. Our intent was to join our people in Montreal, but with our numbers, which is nearly forty, we had to make our way to more established camps. We await arrangements, as so many of our people, for news of settlement. Our uncle and I made our way to Anna and the others to provide rescue that fateful night. Sir John allowed us to gather as many as we might, and we followed our guides dutifully through wild places as we have never known. But most persevered and are rewarded by God for our faith in Him. Please be assured, your brothers and sisters are here. Though Anna is ill with fever, a doctor in the camp tells us it is not fatal, rather brought on by the treacherous journey. Such things we have seen, dear sister . . . though I should imagine you understand as few can, and so I shall not trouble you with the details.

Our mother has followed Father to the prison in Albany to provide such aid as she might. News from spies in the area report he is in ill health. She stays with a Christian family that does not fall under the judgment of the rebels, as they support such a cause, but see no reason why God should not allow aid to other Christian people. We are forever in their debt for this kindness.

Our travels were much maligned by rebels, and our dear neighbour Mr. Silmser did not live to see Quebec, but we are told he did not suffer at the hands of others, but rather, the arduous nature of the journey took its toll on him. He is buried along the trail. His son Nicholas and his family now reside in the camp with our family. We are among friends, dear sister, and take comfort in it.

I pray we shall see one another again when we are settled. Until then, please take care, dear sister, and know we do not forsake our mother and father and will keep them ever under our care.

Your loving brother,
Henrich

I hear Peter speaking to my father-in-law about the news we have received and witness, by the smile upon his face, he is glad for it. While pleased by such news, I wonder if we shall ever see our own dear mama and papa again. So strong he once was, now reduced to linger in destitution at the hands of such men. I must quiet myself, for I feel a familiar scream rising within me, and I cannot succumb to this bitterness. I fold the letter and put it under my mattress, where I shall keep them close in my thoughts and prayers; and attend to my cooking before the children return from visiting our kin a few tents away.

Sitting by the fire, eating his solitary meal, our precious ones now sleeping, Peter suddenly speaks, breaking a most tense silence. "Do not fear. I have secured a billet."

"A billet? But—" I stop, not wanting to distress Peter beyond what he already endures.

"Yes, my dear. We must find a place to live until new land opens up to us. As there are so many arriving daily from our homes, the king's forces are preoccupied with the safety of those yet upon the trail. We have been promised land once there is new surveying done, but this may not be for some time."

"And where are we to live, then?"

"Pointe Claire, downriver. You will be billeted with the Crane family." I am surprised by his reference, which suggests he will not join us.

"Where do you go, then, Peter?"

"We leave forthwith to continue the fight."

I remain silent, not knowing how to express such fear as I have within me that I should be left in this new land with no means of survival, no protector.

"Take heart—it should not be long until we are settled upon our own land once again." He seems hopeful, but unconvinced, for much is unknown.

As the dark of night shades our camp, I hear the frogs' undulating song, which lulls me back to Johnstown, to a time when we found comfort in the familiarity of our life.

CHAPTER 34

We are settled in Pointe Claire in the home of Mr. and Mrs. Crane. Their own children grown, they have taken us in for the duration of our stay. Peter is not with us. We travelled with those charged with our safe delivery to the community, few men being among us. My husband's kin came with us to this community, though they are billeted in other homes. That we will yet have the occasion to see around us the faces of those we love reminds us of the blessings bestowed upon us.

With the advent of fall, which comes sooner and colder than we are used to, my thoughts turn to my kin yet in the camps . . . to my dearest friend and her little Isabel . . . to my dear father and mother. I wonder how they should fare living in such miserable conditions. The winter looms, and as I notice the frost that grows upon the panes of the grand windows in the room I have been given, it is with sorrow that I know my loved ones will not have such comfort as this.

"Mama, look!"

I turn to see Ruby standing in my doorway holding a beautiful lilac dress against her small frame. With a smile that is bright and cheerful, her delight is pure and devoid of the worries that yet trouble us . . . she is radiant.

"Where did you find it?" I inquire, a little concerned that she has trespassed our welcome.

Mrs. Crane, who must have waited in the hallway, comes up behind Ruby and says, "I do hope you do not think me presumptuous, but a young lady such as yours might like a fine dress, after all you—" she stops herself abruptly as though she has said something she should not.

But I smile and put her at ease. "It is most beautiful, and I know my Ruby will revel in it. Thank you for your generosity."

"My dear, it was my own Hannah's dress when she was your Ruby's age, and I am happy that it finds its way to a young one again. Hannah always found much pleasure in her frilly dresses."

"And is your Hannah now married?"

"No, my dear, Hannah left us when she was eleven."

I recognize the familiar distant look, and want to rush to this woman and confess my secret to her, for if anyone should know my pain, it is she. There is a kinship in our loss, but as I do not know her; as I am protective of my memory and selfishly guard it; I simply offer, "I am sorry for your loss."

"It was a very long time ago my dear . . . nearly fifty years, I should think . . ." she pauses, seeming to realize the passing of time. "The enjoyment I now take in sharing her lovely dress with Ruby is a wonderful reminder of what was." She smiles and turns to leave us. "Dinner is served at five."

"I shall come to help at once." My role here is to help this couple with their household. That is to be our repayment for their kindness.

"Not tonight. You have journeyed far; tonight you shall enjoy a proper meal that our cook has prepared."

Such ways, such opulence this home has—so foreign that it makes the distance from our own familiar life further than ever.

Our two rooms are well-appointed, much more so than I believe we need, but I am thankful for it. Ruby and Mathias are each to have their own beds in their room, while Jacob remains with me in mine; he is yet so much a babe.

With the children occupied in their room, and Jacob resting upon my bed, his sleepy eyes fighting to remain open, my thoughts turn to my beloved, for he must be suffering the ills of cold and exposure to the elements . . . and danger. I pray I shall see him again, for I could not bear to part with another so precious to me. Looking to the view outside my window, I take solace in seeing the mountains in the distance across this great river . . . *she* is ever in my thoughts . . .

CHAPTER 35

Spring 1781

The knocks are heavy upon the wooden door as I rush to answer it. Standing before me is a most unexpected sight, and the shock of it sends me falling into his arms. "Peter!" I have not seen him in months. My last sight of him was when he departed with his kin to the shoreline to set off with his battalion the day we journeyed here. I looked back many times to see him in the distance, but he never glanced back at us so that I might see his face one last time, and I was sorry for it.

"Are you here to stay, Peter?" I look up, only to be met by his serious expression.

"No, I am to return by night."

"By night? But we have not seen you in many months; surely they allow you more time?"

"We are only to ensure that our families are well, and we set off once more upon the morn." He does not display any emotion, but as he looks off into the distance, down toward the river, I see he does so to control the emotion that attempts to overtake him.

Sensing that he, as much as I, require aid in doing as we must, I grab his hand and quietly say, "Well, then, we should make the most of our time." My smile seems to provide the reassurance he needs and he enters the house.

"Papa!" The exuberance of my boys in seeing their father is unbridled. Mathias runs to his side, and Peter pulls him close, as Jacob leaps into his arms. I have relinquished my sense of propriety in allowing this, for I do not know when they shall see him again. I know the fleeting nature of life and understand their fear. As Peter's gaze looks back into the hallway behind me, I turn to see the darkened silhouette of our Ruby. She does not move to her father as her brothers have. These past months away from him once again have taken a toll on her. She often wakes in the night screaming his name, and it takes much to reassure her back to sleep. I imagine she believes this to be an apparition before her now.

I move to encourage her, but Peter grabs my arm gently and stops me. He swiftly moves past me into the darkness and, upon reaching Ruby, he crouches down instead of sweeping her up in his arms, as I imagined he would. I can hear his whispered voice: "Hello again, my dear Ruby." There is no response or movement, "I should think you believe me a ghost." Still no sound, but I see her hand reach to touch his face. When she realizes he is truly before her, she lunges to him, wrapping her arms about his neck, sobbing, "Papa, Papa."

The Cranes, having never made his acquaintance, are glad to see the man who heads our family. Mr. Crane takes much pleasure in speaking with Peter about the fight that continues, but as we prepare a celebratory meal in the kitchen, I am glad not to hear the details. Where once I felt it imperative to listen, to know what I may come to expect, this is no longer necessary, for our own bodily survival seems assured in the safety of this community. To know more of what may happen, what my beloved has seen upon his return to our home, would serve no further purpose. It is his safety, and the safety of our kin, that I pray for, not the detail of the perils they face. So much is yet unknown, I dare not think of a future we might not have.

Having enjoyed a meal together, the Cranes rise from the table as we finish. "We are going to take our afternoon rest. It was nice meeting you, dear Mr. Eamer. Please take our good wishes for your well-being with you." Though they often do so, with a smile in her hasty departure, Mrs. Crane proves to be most intuitive about our need to become a family, if only for a few short hours.

"I should like to hear of your adventures upon your return," Mr. Crane says to Peter with a hearty handshake. The two men bow to one another, and the Cranes disappear into their room, shutting the door behind them.

Rising from the table, I begin to clear away our meal, and Peter sits at his leisure watching the mundanity of our life. "Shall we take a walk together? The weather seems favourable, and it may give us a chance for some discussion before I depart." I am happy for his invitation, for I so rarely leave the confines of the house.

As we walk side by side along the shore of the river, we are shy with one another . . . so much time apart, so many experiences apart. Noticing the children ahead of us at some distance, I am fearful of their proximity to the shore. "Do not venture too close to the water's edge, my dears," I call out above the roar of the rushing water, tumbling over ridges in the surface, which creates mesmerizing displays of water splashing about in great white tempests. The river runs swift with the winter's end, so much snow we had this first winter in this land.

" 'Tis very treacherous, indeed; we had much difficulty traversing it but two days ago. We very nearly capsized on more than one occasion."

"You have been in Montreal these two days?"

"Yes; we were resupplying for our next foray."

We walk in silence for a time, watching the children as Jacob darts about, teasing Mathias and Ruby unmercifully with his threats to run to the water. Assured they have corralled him away from the danger, we are at our ease once more.

"It was a lovely meal, dearest. I do hope you find your billet provides some comfort."

"Yes, it is quite comfortable. Much more than I think we need." The thought of him in the open, wild places in the cold of winter, and the misery of the rainy spring, makes our situation even more in contrast to his existence, and I am ashamed of it.

"Do you yet see my mother and sisters?"

"Yes, on occasion. Have your father and brothers joined you in this visit?"

"All but Philip." His voice masks the concern his face cannot.

I am afraid to know what answer may come, but venture, "And what of Philip?"

"He convalesces in Montreal. We very nearly lost him upon the trail home."

"Was he injured?"

"No, a fever swept through our camp. The damp of the rainy weather made for the chill of the night to set the illness. We were stranded many a day with the care of those who had fallen victim."

"I pray he will survive?"

"He will." There is more to this; I hear it in his hesitation, one I have come to know well in these trying times . . .

Grabbing my arm and wrapping it into his own, so that we might be linked now, he stops, looking down at me with a most pitiful expression. Instantly I am struck by a thought: "Is it news of my father? Has he been lost?"

"No, my dear, your father lives. He and your mother made it to Chambly by early December. The imprisonment took a heavy toll on him, and they thought he should not live to see Christmas, but I have just these past few days seen them, and he is well once again."

"Then who, Peter?"

"We have lost Henrich. He did not survive the fever."

So perplexing that I do not cry, for I feel such joy that my father lives, yet it is equalled by the loss of a brother so dear.

"And where is he laid to rest?"

"At Chambly, for he lived until he saw your mother's face and quietly died in her care."

"I should think it brought him some comfort at the end."

"It did."

Alone again. As Peter slips from sight in the heavy rain that makes his presence hazy and then disappear altogether, I do not take to the shelter of the house, but stand and allow the rain to wash over me. And though the deluge makes this night seem bleaker than most, it mimics my sullen mood. I cannot help but imagine what our life should be, and what has come to pass. I cry, for I must seem most ungrateful to our God who has spared us, to wish for such things. Thinking of the faces I shall never again see, I am thankful that mine own shall have such company in their realm.

CHAPTER 36

1783

Lying in my bed, looking out at the early snow that gathers upon my window sill, I see the moon full and bright, casting shadows about me. I feel haunted by the memory of such a moon, the same moon I had once looked upon from my own home so long ago. Three years — it seems such a long time when I see how my children have grown. My Jacob is now older than Mathias was upon our journey. It is a lifetime ago, my existence now, is as though "before" never existed. If it were not for the pain that marks my heart, I should think it only a nightmare . . . but as it is, I know it to be true.

Peter's visits these lonely years in Pointe Claire have been few, as he yet fights with Sir John. He reports little of what he sees, but tells me most certainly that our leaving was a necessity, as nothing remains of the life we knew in Johnstown. Much is destroyed, and hatred for our loyalties has grown. It is now most certain we shall never return, and Sir John begins to arrange for our permanent settlement. The delay has been due to the hope of restitution of our lands; and now there is a lack of men to survey new land, as so many are needed for the fighting. He reminds me always that our patience and loyalty will be rewarded. He is ever kind and gentle with us, which is a miracle of God, for many have become hard and distant.

It has been almost a year since we have seen him, though he sends word on occasion that he is well. His letters are short, as I am sure he writes only to let me know he is alive and his promise to provide for us in the future life is not broken. It is evident from his handwriting that he has not always fared so well, but he is alive, and we can hope that what he promises may yet be.

The forfeit of our life in Johnstown has so much altered my purpose that I often feel lost. Though I am yet a mother, my children grow, and I am now left alone in my bed at night, the children sharing a room and delighting in the adventures they find down by the river with their cousins and new-found friends. I fill my days with servitude to the Cranes, which I happily do, for they are kind and generous with us; but it is not as it should be. Where once I have had the joy of being a wife who found delight in maintaining my own home, cooking meals for my family upon my own hearth, mending by the fire as I rocked upon my chair, engaged in casual conversation with my beloved, this is no more . . . nor have I had the joy of welcoming more children.

Always I speak to mine own in the dark of the night, when the tears of despair roll down my cheeks, and I remember having her in my arms, sensing her warmth against me. I see her face as clearly as ever, and I take some comfort in the babe I will always have.

"A treaty has been signed. Hostilities end." Such news, such news! I feel a great weight has lifted, and I see the face of my beloved, hoping he comes to us now.

My sister-in-law Rebekah, who has waited for news of Martin these many months, tentatively asks, "When shall they return home, Mother?"

"Soon, I should think, as this Treaty of Paris, as they call it, was signed on September third," my mother-in-law says, referring to a copy of the *Gazette* that she has received from the MacDonalds, with whom she billets. These many years, they have allowed us to meet at their home each Sunday afternoon in deference to my mother-in-law's role as our elder—and often only guiding presence—as we wait. September third. There has been peace these many days, and we still do not see our men return to us. A most dreadful thought enters my mind, but I do not entertain it; I could not bear it.

Sensing our fears, our mother-in-law cheerfully announces, "Take heart, my dears, for now our lives may begin anew." Her faith has been unfaltering, and though I may ever want for such hope, there are reasons I cannot wholeheartedly embrace it.

These nine weeks, we have waited, and no word has arrived. I look out my window at the coming of winter: drifts of snow gather upon the shore, and the river slows as it freezes and crusts upon the banks. *When will they come to us, then?* I hear a faint knock at my door, an unusual occurrence that stirs me from my solitary places. *I must have forgotten the time, and she comes to beckon me to my work.* Hurriedly, I rise from my chair set by the window and open the door, only to be met by Mrs. Crane's broad smile, which signals she has good news to share. Suddenly my beloved appears. "I am discharged."

CHAPTER 37

Spring 1784

We have languished these four years in Pointe Claire, and though our life has been made richer by the new friends we have made, it is time for us to make our home as a family, independent of the kindness of others. Peter has served the king well, and now a settlement is to open up to the West, and we are finally able to draw lots. We are to be rewarded for our loyalty. At one time, the reward, even as it is, would have been much too insignificant for our sacrifices; but now, as our children grow, and the immensity of my pain and loss distances itself from me, I believe we have seen enough tragedy to fill our lifetime, and we look forward to what comes.

Sitting in the front room of the Crane home, the men, including my husband's kin, discuss our resettlement with Mr. Crane. As I make our meal, I can hear my father-in-law's confident voice: "We will settle along the boundary, along the shores of the river, should we need to defend against attack."

To hear that we settle along such natural beauty primarily as a defence against uncertain attack saddens me. I pray it will not mark our existence . . . perhaps God will spare us, and this shall not come to pass. So much has happened . . . I am glad to know we should have a legacy for our children, that they should have this land as their future. *I pray, dear God, it shall be so, for once I believed it to be in our beloved Johnstown.*

We are to journey to this place, along the mighty St. Lawrence, which I have come to love, and we are to live in tents as once before and then draw our lot. It seems fitting that this new settlement is to be called "New Johnstown." Perhaps this signals the hope that we can recreate what has been lost these many years . . . though I know it cannot, for even now, part of me resides in the past, along the trail, and faded memories of my tree haunt me yet. For a moment I dwell in "before" but am quickly brought back to reality by my beloved's exuberant voice: "Captain Sherwood reports the land is good, and we have one year to establish a homestead. It will be exhausting work, but the reward shall be great. Should we meet this condition, the land is ours."

Lying in our bed together, my head upon his chest, I think of the journey we will undertake in the morn . . . "Do my kin join us on our new land?"

"Yes, our people gather once more. We shall build our Johnstown anew."

"I shall never be able to repay your kindness, my dear Mrs. Crane," I say with some sadness at our leaving. To wish for something so ardently, to finally have my own home once again, stirs within me a bewildering convergence of sentiments.

"It was a pleasure I shall always remember. The joy of having life brought back into our home has shored us up and given us fond memories on which to ponder."

Our young man Mathias offers his hearty handshake to the now elderly Mr. Crane, and he bows in reverence to Mrs. Crane, picking up our meagre possessions as he leaves. Jacob, our spirited one — who seemingly remembers nothing of our journey here — simply waves a friendly goodbye from atop the wagon that carries our provisions for our new life.

Ruby always having had a special place in her affections, Mrs. Crane hands her a small, beaded clutch, which she opens to reveal an array of colourful ribbons. Smiling at the surprise, Ruby embraces Mrs. Crane tenderly. Theirs has been a special bond. Though I was not privy to its nature, I believe my insightful, pensive girl understood that Mrs. Crane needed her as much as we needed them. With a tearful, "Please write to me from time to time, my dear Ruby," Mrs.

Crane wipes a solitary tear from her cheek and regains her dignified composure.

As I turn back to see Peter making his farewells, he hands Mr. Crane a small pouch, payment for our recent months' stay. Though I knew it to be so, Sir John having arranged restitution to our billets, I had not yet had the occasion to witness the exchange. While it does not diminish my affections for the Cranes, it makes me happy that we should come to rely on ourselves once again.

We set off as a great caravan of people, we who are called "refugees." We are given a horse, wagon, and supplies; and rely wholly on our hope and fortitude.

I am with child once more. It seems God has answered my prayer in ensuring no child should be born to us while we are without a home. And now, as I look back to the last hints of Pointe Claire upon the horizon, I take heart that this time shall be different, for though I do not know what awaits us in the land that we journey to, we are under the protection of Peter, and I need not assume his role as once I did. I do not like to think upon our exodus and what has been lost . . . her small face shall always provide me comfort, and though her life was forfeited for our loyalty, her existence, though shrouded in secrecy, is my private joy and becomes my hope for what may come.

There is no evidence of man, here. It is a wild and untamed land. We live among the Mohawk, and though we might not see them, they are near, as was always our Mohawk guide upon the trail. I do not fear them as do some. When one has faced the gravity of such a situation, when fear has been your whole existence, and where once you may have thought it unbearable — this I have lived, and survived . . . *survived.* Little of who I was or how I defined my existence remains, and yet there is a foundation on which to begin anew. It is faint, but it is present.

CHAPTER 38

1787

"Good morning, my dear." I smile as I walk toward Peter standing at the rail fence he is yet building. I wake as in the time "before," and go to see him walking his land in the early mornings. Though it is not yet fully cultivated, he takes pride that much progress has been made these three years, and we are now able to feed our growing family from its bounty. Having fulfilled our obligation to clear the land within a year of our arrival, he once again feels the satisfaction of owning land and working it as he wishes.

"It looks like you have much help this morning," I say, looking toward Daniel, who seems to listen attentively in a corn field that is just beginning to sprout, as Mathias and Jacob instruct their young brother on how to check the crop. Daniel, our boy born before our first winter in this place, knows only this life. His birth signalled a truly new beginning, as he is our first child born on this land. He shall never be of the Johnstown we once loved so well . . . I still love so well. Even *mine own* belongs to a time lost to us. Our ties to that life are broken.

Turning to watch them in their instruction, Peter's pride is evident. "He is eager to learn, and his brothers are becoming wise in the ways of farming. I should think they will be very successful when they embark on their own."

"It is under your instruction that they are so." I am glad to give Peter so many sons to carry on our traditions.

"Your trees come into bloom. You may see your first harvest this year."

I glance at the grove of small apple trees full of delicate pink blossoms, planted by my beloved as a most special gift; he does not know their beauty is tinged with melancholy. "They are lovely. I look forward to tasting their sweet fruit."

"I go to rejoin our young men and see what wisdom they have imparted." As he walks to meet our boys, the sun glints off the river in the distance, catching my attention. Such a familiar sight — a beautiful sight that I cannot yet allow myself simply to enjoy, for its familiarity to the place where we come from reminds me ever of home. Peter does not understand the pensiveness that at times overtakes me, though I feel his gaze often set upon me when this happens. Perhaps he fears the answer, and therefore does not venture the question. As my affection for this place grows, I feel torn between two places . . . two times. I shall never forget "before": the places of my childhood, the places of my life beginning with Peter, the sense of living in a utopia. Perhaps my memories have grown sweeter with time, but I do not think so. For even then, I knew we were most blessed by God.

As my children play amongst the fallen trees of our land, there is always a ghost among them. I see her in my mind's eye playing with them, laughing with them . . . and always as I kiss them good night, singing the songs that they love so well, I think of her and imagine kissing her upon the softness of her cheek, always feeling the warmth of life as I once did.

"Shall I rouse Elizabeth, Mama?"

Stirred from my thoughts, I turn to see Ruby with Elias in her arms. Not but a year old, he endeavours to bound from her to join his father and brothers, whom he points to most fervently, calling "Papa, Papa!"

"Yes, my dear." Ruby stands tall within the shadowed doorway, a reflection of her papa in both stature and manner. She is a most cherished companion in my work. "I will dress her then come to prepare their meal at once."

"Yes, dearest. I shall come to help."

Upon reaching her, I gather Elias in my arms and lift him over my shoulder so that he may yet see his beloved papa in the field. Relieved of such a busy one, Ruby most dutifully moves to the children's room, calling back, "I will join you in just a moment." Having come so close together, our babies require much effort, thankfully leaving little time for such sad reflection.

I walk to my father's homestead, which sits directly upon the shores of the great river. His service to the king was rewarded with a lot that provides all of us much abundance from the use of it, and bounty that comes from its depths. Though it places him in harm's way should we be attacked from our once neighbours, he fears not, for he is most ardent in his defence of this land. His many months of lingering in the decrepit prison of the rebels, brought to bear at the hands of his once fellow compatriots, has left a mark of bitterness in him. He is ever just with us in his community, but when conversing about the land across this river, he holds no affection in his heart for their plight.

As my mother, sisters, and I gather to wash by the river's edge, our men go to help my father in clearing the land for further cultivation. Our oldest boys are alongside, learning the ways that will see them live off the land and provide for their own families in the years to come.

"Our place on this land is most assured now," my mother says, looking upon her many grandchildren who run about. "So much has occurred. We are to be thankful for so many blessings — the children who have been born to us in this place signal that our hope for a future on this land begins to take hold, and they shall flourish with the abundance that this land provides."

My sisters and I do not answer, but simply look up from our washing and smile at one another. My dear mama is pensive and speaks as though to herself and God alone. With our people once again living as neighbours, the marriages of so many who were but children upon the trail many years before, and the arrival of countless children, we have grown and begin to see the semblance of a community emerge from the dense forests that met us upon our arrival.

CHAPTER 39

November 10, 1813

War finds us once again.

As predicted many years ago, our men are forced to take up arms in defence against invaders. We do not fight our neighbours and kin this time, though once we may have called them so. Our thirty-three years on this land have separated us from these usurpers of our peaceful life here. Our communities are put at risk as we hear of fearsome battles being fought along the length of our beautiful river and beyond. My boys fight at their father's side, and it now seems my efforts to shield them from the evils of the world we left behind have failed. I had merely delayed what was destined to be their fate.

This war sees those the children of our exodus face the horrors of defending what they believe to be rightful and just. I think of what may be sacrificed in this defence, and pray this will not be so once more. Even grown as they are, their care is ever in my prayers.

Alone I wait in the silence . . .

My beloved would love a night such as this. The sky in varying shades of slate blue from the horizon, with just a hint of the past day appearing as a ribbon of soft, pink light at the very edge where the land and sky meet, progressively darkens as I look up at the stars, now appearing above and signalling the coming of night. The only sounds are the familiar, undulating chirps of the frogs at the river. They seem less a multitude of sounds, but rather, in their unison, as though they are one. It is a sound that generally provides comfort; but not tonight.

Occasional haunting sounds of a loon calling its mate magnify the emptiness of the night. The dampness is permeating my light woollen shawl. I pull it tighter to ward off the loneliness and chill that now envelop me. With one last, strained effort to hear any sound in the darkness—any man-made sound—I reluctantly retreat into the warmth of the house.

Is it real, or is it wishful thinking? The sounds of horses' hooves and men's voices are so faint. I strain to listen, above the crackle of the fire . . . yes, it is men. I am sure of it.

Swinging open hard, the door hits the wall with a loud BANG! Men pour into the room as a jumble of bodies, carrying the limp body of a man, yelling for water, whisky, and sheets as they carry him into the adjoining room. In his unconscious state, he hits the bed with a thud and lies motionless, as though dead.

The strong, metallic smell of blood, salty sweat, and the sulphur of gunpowder is overwhelming in the small, darkened room, only dimly lit by the solitary oil lamp in the corner. The flickering of the light casts shadows that dance about the walls in strange configurations.

Surrounding me are faces barely recognizable as men. A thick coat of dark, brown mud covers every inch of them, but the body on the bed I know, regardless of the current state he is in. Alive! At least he is alive! A sense of relief engulfs me.

I am pushed forcefully aside by a large man whose face is coated with cracking, dry mud. He takes charge, barking orders in a stern, unwavering voice: "Water, sheets, knife. Hold him down men, lest he awaken while I remove the bullet." Though a mass of men gather around the body, he is still visible, the blood oozing from the wound in the upper left arm dark, almost black, and thick as molasses. The only evidence of its being blood is the red stain, which is growing against the few remaining white scraps of shirt adhering to the wound itself and the now torn bits of sheet being applied and thrown to the floor in the chaos.

The sound of the knife tip hitting metal . . . the deep moaning of the body on the bed . . . the extreme heat of the room . . . the overwhelming smells . . . helplessness . . .

"It doesn't look like he's going to make it," says the man who has taken out the bullet, his brow deeply furrowed with unease that his efforts were to no avail. "He's lost a lot of blood on the rough ride back here, and the fever has already started. There's no telling if the infection can be stopped. I think all the pieces of shirt were removed, but the mud and the grass we were fighting in . . ." he trails off, seeming to be lost in his own thoughts and obvious exhaustion. Facing me, so close, I am frightened. "Well, there is no saying what we were in. Best to sit close, in case he comes to. But I would suggest prayer is all we have on our side at this point."

With little more to be done, the men file out one by one, each giving me a mournful nod as they leave our home.

Quiet.

Yearning to tell him — I wonder if he can hear me? I am desperate . . . unsure . . . sensing the end may be near. In a hesitant, whispered voice, I begin. "Peter? Peter. There is something I must confess."

He moans so strangely, as though he fights death itself, but I continue.

"Peter, there was another—"

Wild blue-grey eyes pop open.

CHAPTER 40

Sitting in the shade of my apple trees, I look over the life we have built—the home we have found. Our children are grown, and we know the delight of grandchildren, and satisfied with the life I have led, am ready for what is to come.

"My dear, I am dying."

Peter's face takes on the familiar look of so many times in our life of both helplessness and resignation. "I know, Catrina. Is there something I might do to provide any comfort?"

I look toward the mountains that hold mine own in their care and feel no need to provide reason for it, but simply ask, "I should like to be buried in sight of the mountains at the shore of the river." As I look at the silvery river that separates my two homes, I yearn to take my rest there, for though we were pushed out, I do not love my Johnstown less for the troubles it has seen.

Breathlessly, I continue, "I shall like . . . I shall like to have an . . . apple blossom from my tree . . . placed on my breast . . . before I am put . . . in the ground."

"But my dear, perhaps you will live to see the fruit the trees bear." His yearning for what cannot be is just as I had felt many years ago upon our exodus when Mathias believed there to be hope in returning to our home.

Gently I grab his hand, and look into his eyes, as blue-grey as ever they were, and as I had with Mathias, made him understand. "I shall not, my beloved."

"I am sorry . . . to leave you."

Peter gathers me close, and though my bodily pain is overcoming me, and I struggle to catch my breath, I take comfort in his warmth, for I grow cold.

"Catrina, the children have gathered and wish to say their good-byes." As I look into his eyes, tears welling, he is doing as he must, as we all must. Our time together, alone as man and wife comes to an end . . . such love I have known. I smile at him, and the children quietly enter my chamber, which is dark. "Open . . . the curtains so that . . . it might be . . . brighter." He squeezes my hand, and gives a tender smile; I shall always rejoice in his nature, for it has remained intact. I want to see the faces of my children, now grown as they are, in the lightness that reflects the joy they bring to my life, and not have the shroud of death hanging over us in these last moments together. Too much darkness has marked our existence. As the light floods into the room, the faces that surround me come into full view and I am filled with peace.

Where fear once filled me with what might come, and I despaired over what was lost, hope now fills my heart, and that time of strife finally comes to rest. My hope is renewed and I look forward to where I go, knowing my only reason for being on this earth was to bear these children, love this man, and ensure all of their survival as I was able . . . My work is done . . . and though they will mourn my passing, they will live on.

Ruby, sitting at my side, holds my hand, and Peter holds the other. I hear her singing to me, the songs of my childhood; the songs of their childhood. One by one, my children come to me and kiss me most tenderly upon my forehead, and I struggle to remain conscious so that I might remember the warmth of their lips upon me as I take my leave of them. I cannot catch my breath but so wish to give each a farewell that they might hear me utter their name once more, they look as children to me for guidance, so lost are my precious ones that I must endure to give each a goodbye. I see her small face appear amongst the others . . . the pain leaves me . . . Looking at these loving faces that surround me, I cannot help but smile. I am assured they are all well and I go to see her again . . . *"mine own."*

CHAPTER 41

David? . . . David?

This fog is so thick . . . where am I? It's cold, and there's a strong smell of pine in the air. I love this smell; it reminds me of the mountains and the pine forests we hike through . . . I must be outdoors.

Good, the sky is starting to brighten; maybe I'll be able to see where I am once the sun rises. It's so strange . . . I don't feel scared . . . I just wish I could see through this fog.

Brrr. Even though the grass at my feet is nice and soft, it's cold. Where are my shoes?

I don't know if it's just getting brighter or the fog is starting to lift . . . who's that? I see a figure beginning to take form, but only in silhouette. It's not moving, and I don't feel I should run—it's just standing there.

It sounds so incredible listening to all the birds beginning to greet the day, more every second. It has to be early morning, because I can see a brightening in one particular spot in the sky where the sun is going to rise in front of me. Where am I?

I hear a faint sound . . . It's hard to hear over the sounds of all the birds—there must be thousands, and with a red-winged blackbird close by, it's hard to hear anything but its call.

There it is again. I think it's coming from the direction of the person standing so still in front of me. It sounds like—like a low and melancholy humming, with a vaguely familiar sound, but I'm sure I don't know the words.

With a flash of light, the sun crests a mountain ridge in the distance, and the fog disappears almost entirely, leaving just enough to give this place an other-worldly feel. As I look at the figure, I can see it's a woman, younger than me, maybe in her mid-twenties, golden hair tied loosely, allowing some of the soft waves to fall about her face and shoulders. I can't see her face because she is looking at a small bundle she is cradling in her arms. It looks like it's wrapped with some sort of . . . grey shawl . . . and I can see a subtle movement from it.

I know where I am.

This familiar mountain ridge, overlooking an endless view of mountain ridges; sky the colour of early morning in brilliant hues of pink and orange, I am an observer here, this is a dream . . . I know where I am.

I look back at her as she holds her baby and am met by blue eyes, strikingly the same colour as the sky now. She pulls back the shawl and shows me that she is singing to a small baby, eyes open and trained on her mother. She looks back down at her daughter, and I see a small, growing smile. Lifting her head to look at me again, she is beautiful . . . and at peace. We gaze at each other with understanding. All has been revealed; all has been shared. "Mine own," and her mother, my fifth great-grandmother, Maria Catrina Gallinger Eamer, have found peace and each other.

WAKING TO THE FAMILIAR, soothing sounds of birds outside her window — the red-winged blackbird's song standing out among all others — a tranquility she had not experienced over the past few weeks washed over Eliza. In sharing her secret, Maria Catrina had reached through time and staked a claim in this world for her beloved namesake. The baby so long ago buried in the wilds of the forest upon a mountain ridge; a baby only ever known to her mother — though once her existence was almost revealed in a dark room full of the smells of blood and war — took her rightful place in the Eamer family. The bond between mother and child, regardless of time together, was etched upon the soul; the bonds between grandmothers and their descendants were equally so, for Eliza was the daughter of the sons and daughters who enjoyed the warm embrace of their mother in life.

In a final act of gratitude for the journey Eliza had shared with her great-grandmother, she decided to pay her respects along the shoreline at the St. Lawrence Valley Cemetery, itself a result of relocating eighteen historic burial grounds lost during the Seaway project, a place where she had seen the modern stone that commemorated her grandmother's beloved "Mama"—a place close to her people and their history.

Driving along the familiar, winding river road, thinking back on all the characters she had met both in person and through dream, Eliza came to realize they were characters in her own story—that she was connected to the history in books but had discovered the humanity in the history by experiencing unknown chapters and people. She thought of a recent public radio documentary that had used the phrase, "the emotional histories we inherit." The power of the statement had played over and over in her mind in the past week, and though unsure if the intended context was that our histories can be emotional, it did not matter, as there was truth for her when hearing it. Emotional histories are embedded in our DNA, interwoven in our makeup; although the legacy of our ancestors could not always be explored in genealogical research or history books, they resided within us, sometimes revealing themselves through the unknown strength we might find to face adversity, the feeling of being connected to places we should not know . . . or through dreams.

The presence of the Mohawk guide, though nameless in her dreams, stuck with her. He had been called "Indian," which offended her modern beliefs. She was friends with, and had deep respect for, the Mohawk people and appreciated what his role had been in the story. This silent figure had been forced into an impossible choice. She knew he was comfortable in the surroundings because it was his home—the trees, the animals, even the well-worn trails were the friends of his childhood, his life. In this place so sacred and loved, people with differing customs and sensibilities turned on one another, as did the Oneidas and Tuscarora of the Iroquois alliance, aligned with the rebels or "patriots" of so much history she had read. The Mohawk was forced to fear his once-trusted allies. There was no clear winner in this history. "The first civil war" sadly would be dwarfed by what was to come during the time of the descendants of this first round.

The colonial experience and its impact were fresh in a modern context of the world. Her friends the Mohawk people now lived on small, segregated tracts of land. Her part in the revealed history would have been easy to shy away from — to only explore, and believe, the shaded versions of glory and triumph; but her grandmother had allowed her to experience the complex, complicated truth.

Her German ancestors had fled their home country for a new world, a new start within lands already established by people who lived on, and loved, the land; then helped colonize these places, only to be forced out when the colony matured, seeking its own identity. Could she feel proud, or would guilt override this? She came to realize that history just "is"; it cannot be changed to suit modern sensibilities. When she looked back on all those from whom she was descended: German Palatine / Loyalists / Colonial Americans . . . "Refugees," French, Scottish, even happily finding two Native women in her genealogy, Eliza wondered if she would be able to reconcile her place in this country and history — good and bad.

Now standing in the quiet of the graveyard, the world was enveloped in the haziness and surreal nature that only dusk can bring, Eliza felt connected to the ghosts of the river — the places, experiences, and the people that now lay beneath it. On its unnatural course, it swallowed the land, cutting the connection of all future generations to these places. No longer could they sit at the graves of their ancestors. The river was the divide of history and time made permanent.

Familiar and calling, her yearning for the other side of the shore, she now understood, was the memory left by those who had gone before, and when the soul recognizes these places, it is undeniable and not to be explained away by rational thought. Her dreams had been the mark left by Maria Catrina. As she looked over the wide divide of water to the mountains, Eliza knew Catrina had been comforted, knowing that the mountains that cradled her baby were in sight of her own final resting place.

She had never thought about the Loyalists much beyond the labels in museum displays, but the truth was that the human horror and sacrifice was real, raw, and unimaginable. The incredible saga — the exodus — of the Loyalist families and their fortitude instilled a sense of pride in her; in particular, the strength of the women, whose stories are so rarely told.

Women in her family tree had been like shadows in the lives of their men; yet, the strength demonstrated when called upon rivalled that of the men, whose glorious battles were so often told. The truth revealed, Eliza reflected, that women reassured terrified children; women fought valiantly in defence of their loved ones; women endured suffering and strife with dignity; women comforted the dying, ensuring that their last sight in this world was one of caring and the gentleness of a mother comforting her dying baby. To think that woman was her ancestor was inspiring. Though Maria Catrina Gallinger Eamer had lingered in the shadows of the family tree — in the fabric of her own DNA — Eliza realized she, and the other Loyalist women of history, are the unsung, and too often forgotten, heroes of stories. They nurtured families so that they might survive, and 200 years on, the flags that flew were now a reminder to Eliza of the whole story. So while the story started with Peter, Maria Catrina stepped out of the shadow of her husband's life and took her rightful place at his side as one of the two people who built a family of thousands.

In all that had been revealed, the horror of decisions that had to be made, Eliza fully understood that strength of the connection of Loyalist descendants to their past. In the courage to stand for what they believed to be the right course of action, the only decision that could be made, they had sacrificed home, and sometimes family, to stand by their convictions. The legacy of the Loyalists, she concluded, was not the flags that fly in commemoration, but rather what was being commemorated: the sacrifice, the strength, the hope for a home—for peace.

Looking out over the water as night quickly fell, Eliza placed on the water a single pink apple blossom she had plucked from a nearby tree and let it float away. As it was pulled out ever farther over the place where Maria Catrina rested in the embrace of the river, it slowly faded from sight just as Eliza's eyes met the horizon and the mountains in the distance. With tears streaming down her cheeks, she whispered, "Thank you."

The tender scene she had been witness to at the end was a gift in understanding that the voices of our grandmothers carry forward, and if we are quiet, our minds still, our hearts open—we hear them.

Epilogue

WITH THEIR ANNUAL summer vacation upon them, Eliza, the resident "travel planner," had decided that their meandering road to their destination should take them into the Mohawk Valley and Johnstown, before heading east to the coast of Maine.

The Adirondack Mountains they travelled through en route had new meaning. They had always held Eliza in awe of their majestic, natural beauty, with forests of pine and birch and vistas of the ranges that seemed to be endless, but now she wondered where a small grave lay within them. Her connection to the experiences witnessed in these places was strong, and with the GPS indicating they were within five minutes of Johnson Hall State Historic Site, in the heart of the land of her ancestors, she felt the roots begin to take hold.

As Johnson Hall came into sight, the images in her dreams mixed with reality. She could almost see the great Iroquois conferences and the reading of the Declaration of Independence upon the stairs of this historic mansion, now directly before her.

Once parked, David readied the kids to visit the site, knowing Eliza needed a minute to process what she was seeing and experiencing. He, more than anyone, knew that Eliza *felt* her history, and since she had shared her dreams with him, he knew this was an emotional stop.

Opening the door, Eliza took in the fragrant, warm air mixed with scents of freshly mowed grass, flowers from the abundant gardens . . . and pine. Swivelling around in her seat, she let both feet hit the ground—and at once was "home."

INSPIRED BY TRUE EVENTS

THIS BOOK WAS INSPIRED by real individuals—Peter Eamer and Maria Catrina Gallinger—within the author's genealogy. It should be noted that this is a *fact-based fiction*, and dates and events relating to the family have been changed to accommodate this story. The history in which this story is set has been extensively researched to ensure historical accuracy and to illustrate the distressing times prior to and during the American Revolution for the people of the Mohawk Valley.

This fictionalized plight of Maria Catrina would have been experienced by countless women ensuring the safety of their families through the wilderness that separated one beloved home for a new and unknown future in British territory—now Canada.

HISTORICAL TIMELINE

Around 1708: First mass migration of Palatines to American colonies. This group of people originated from the Palatinate or German Pfalz region (Southern Rhine region) of Germany. It should be noted that *Palatines* also came from other regions such as the Netherlands (Calvinists) and France (Huguenots: French Protestants), as they had fled to the Palatinate, many to escape religious persecution.

1712: First settlement of Palatines in the Schoharie and Mohawk Valleys (Province of New York).

1775–83: American Revolution or U.S. War of Independence.

May 19, 1776: Having received word of his impending arrest, Sir John Johnson flees Johnstown with an estimated 170–200 tenants and friends. They trek through the Adirondack Mountains to Quebec. He leaves behind his pregnant wife, Lady Johnson, and their two young children, stating that travel would be too arduous for them. She was later arrested and sent to Albany. She gave birth to a son, John, on October 7, 1776.

June 15, 1776: Sir John Johnson and his followers arrive in Quebec said to be "starving and in poor condition."

June 19, 1776: Sir John Johnson raises the King's Royal Regiment of New York (KRRNY) in Quebec.

July 4, 1776: Declaration of Independence adopted by the Continental Congress in Philadelphia.

July 8, 1776: First public reading of the Declaration in Philadelphia (first newspaper printing of the Declaration in the *Philadelphia*

Evening Post, July 6, 1776). The Declaration was then read publicly throughout the colonies.

August 6, 1777: Battle of Oriska (Oriskany). This bloody battle saw the Tryon County (Mohawk Valley) militia attempt to aid the Americans at a standoff at Fort Schuyler (later Fort Stanwix). Approximately a force of 700, under the command of Sir John Johnson, met the militia en route to the fort. The majority of Sir John's forces were made up of their Native allies. It is estimated that 500 Tryon County militia were killed, captured, or wounded, and about fifty Natives and a number of Loyalists killed.

Note: Though neutrality was attempted by many, e.g., the Palatine colonists, it should be noted that the Six Nations of the Iroquois (Mohawk, Onondaga, Oneida, Seneca, Tuscarora, and Cayuga) also experienced a split during the American Revolution, with the Oneida and Tuscarora giving the majority of their support to the American cause.

May 21, 1780: Sir John Johnson and his men return to Johnstown, Province of New York, to lay siege to the valley and their former home. They also rescued Loyalists during their various forays.

July 13, 1780: King's Royal Regiment of New York (KRRNY) 2nd Battalion raised.

September 3, 1783: Treaty of Paris signed, ending hostilities between Great Britain and the United States and recognizing American independence.

1775–83: Exodus of United Empire Loyalists to British territories in British North America (Quebec and Nova Scotia at the time), the Caribbean, and Britain.[1]

1784: New settlements in British North America are surveyed and granted to United Empire Loyalists. The author's ancestors, the inspiration for this book, settled along the St. Lawrence River throughout the historic Stormont, Dundas, and Glengarry

---

[1] "Historians estimate that 10 to 15 percent of the population of the Thirteen Colonies — some 250,000 people — opposed the revolution; some passively, others by speaking out, spying, or fighting against the rebels." http://www.uelac.org/PDF/loyalist.pdf.

counties, including New Johnstown—now modern-day Cornwall, Ontario.

Committee of Safety: Though in existence before the American Revolution, during this time, these committees acted as the local government representing local interests, discussing and sharing news of current issues, and took charge of their militias. Those who were neutral or known Loyalists were often called in for questioning.

About the Author

WITH DEEP ancestral roots in New France/Quebec, Upper Canada/ Ontario, and colonial America, Jennifer is interested in exploring the human story within this rich history. Combining her passion and experience in writing, education, history, and genealogy, she writes fact-based, historical fiction that engages readers in "discovering the humanity in the history." A dynamic and knowledgeable speaker, Jennifer is a sought-after presenter at historical, literary and community events.

Jennifer holds the hereditary title of UE as a proven descendant of the United Empire Loyalists who settled in Upper Canada (modern-day Ontario, Canada) during the 1780s.

Shadows in the Tree is her second novel.

Other works by the author:

www.jenniferdebruin.com

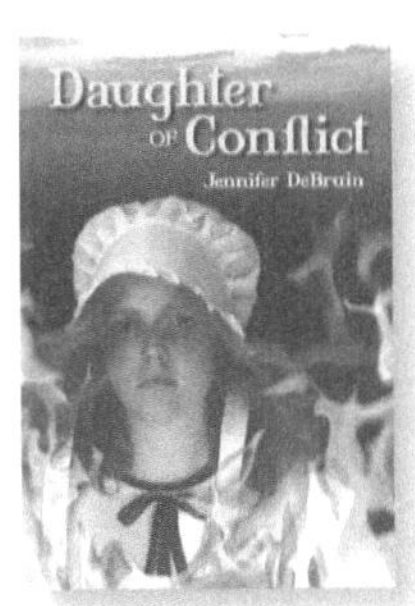